A
HARLEQUIN
Book

ISLE OF POMEGRANATES

by

IRIS DANBURY

HARLEQUIN BOOKS

WINNIPEG ● CANADA

First published in 1969 by Mills & Boon Limited,
50 Grafton Way, Fitzroy Square, London, England.

SBN 373-01372-8

© Iris Danbury 1969

Harlequin Canadian edition published February, 1970
Harlequin U.S. edition published May, 1970

Printed in Canada

1372

CHAPTER ONE

On her way home from the office Felicity Hilton stopped to buy chops and tomatoes and, in a burst of extravagance, a half-bottle of Chianti.

Compensation? she mused. For what? For saying good-bye to a dream, perhaps.

She hurried home to the small flat in a tall Victorian house in a square behind Bayswater Road. Trevor, her young brother, was lying in an armchair, his dark glasses effectively masking whether he were asleep or not.

'Hallo!' he greeted her. 'You're late, aren't you?'

'Am I?' She stayed a few moments before her bedroom mirror, tidying her red-gold hair. 'I had to go to the shops.'

She cooked the meal, poured out glasses of wine.

'What are we celebrating?' Trevor asked.

'Oh, nothing in particular,' she answered lightly. 'I thought it might cheer you up.'

'Or are you the one who needs cheering up?' he queried with a smile. 'Not still pining after Philip, are you? If you ask me, I think it's a damn good job you're rid of him.'

'No, all that's forgotten,' she assured him. But, indeed, nobody had asked Trevor his opinion when Philip had told her only a fortnight ago that he was going to marry some-one else.

'Anyone I know?' She had tried to sound casual.

'Yes, Beryl.'

'Beryl!' The name had been forced out of her. 'Why, I——'

'I know. You introduced us at someone's party,' agreed Philip. 'But I'd no idea then of falling in love with her.' After a silence, he had continued, 'The truth is, Felicity, that I'm tired of being put off over and over again for the sake of that brother of yours. I don't exactly want to start

5

my married life with you dividing your attention between him and me. If that sounds selfish, I'm sorry.'

'If Trevor doesn't take care now, he'll go blind,' she had told Philip. 'But he won't always be like that. We hope that some new treatment——'

'He can see a pretty girl fast enough,' muttered Philip. 'I've asked you a dozen times to let him go to——'

'Yes, I know. To let him go to some institution or home for the blind,' she finished. 'I couldn't do that.'

'I wanted to marry you, Felicity, not your brother as well, and in the meantime, I've grown very fond of Beryl.'

Felicity had never been formally engaged to Philip. There had been only an understanding that some time in the future, when Trevor was no longer in danger of threatened blindness, they would marry. She could hardly blame Philip for being impatient. He had waited for more than two years, but now she had lost him to one of her own friends. Yet the gap he had left in her life was almost unbearable and she longed to get away somewhere and start afresh.

Today that chance had been offered her, but she could not take it because Trevor must come first. So now it was goodbye again to a dream.

She worked as secretary to one of the directors of a company engaged in export and import business with Sweden and Norway, and today her boss, Mr. Firth, had introduced her to a tall, fair young man, Dr. Hendrik Johansen, whom she imagined was a representative of one of the Swedish trading companies.

'Dr. Johansen has a proposition which concerns you, Miss Hilton.' Mr. Firth had smiled encouragingly at her. 'He would like to—er—sort of borrow you—as secretary for a while.'

'Yes?'

'I have a clinic on a small island in the Adriatic off the Italian coast. A beautiful place and excellent climate, but there is not much gay life.'

'You would want me to work there? For how long?' she

6

asked.

Dr. Johansen shrugged. 'Perhaps six months. Maybe more.'

Felicity's quickened interest immediately faded. 'I'm sorry. I couldn't be away from London for so long. I have responsibilities here.'

'Of course, Miss Hilton needs a little time to consider the plan,' broke in Mr. Firth. 'And I can tell you, Johansen, I'm none too keen to part with her even for six months.'

The two men went out to lunch together, and Felicity walked to her usual cafeteria in Eastcheap. As she mechanically ate her lunch, unaware of the buzz of conversation, the stuffy, food-scented atmosphere, she wrestled with this new problem.

If only she were free and could accept this exciting offer of new surroundings, new faces, she might learn to quell the agonising ache that had been her constant companion since she and Philip had parted.

But how could she desert her eighteen-year-old brother who suffered from an obscure eye disease that threatened total blindness even before he had begun to think of a career?

When Mr. Firth returned from lunch, Felicity told him that she could not possibly consider Dr. Johansen's suggestion.

'Because of your brother, I suppose? I guessed as much.'

'You know that we've no parents. Trevor has no one but me and he can't fend for himself.'

'Pity.' Mr. Firth twirled in his revolving chair. 'You could do with a long, working holiday in a sunny climate. You can't sacrifice all your life even to your brother. If nothing can be done for him to prevent his blindness, then he ought to start training for something.'

Felicity said nothing. The subject was closed.

Now, as she cleared away the dishes and washed up, she put away from her the last shred of regret. She hoped that Dr. Johansen would find someone equally suitable.

But next morning Mr. Firth called her in to meet the

doctor again. 'I don't know why I'm being so noble in depriving myself of the best secretary I've ever had,' he began, 'but I've explained about your brother and Dr. Johansen believes he can help you.'

'One of my colleagues on the island is an eye specialist,' the doctor said eagerly. 'Indeed, that is not surprising, for we have many specialists in different fields. But my friend might be able to prescribe the right treatment.'

Felicity looked dubious. 'But the fees?' She had already spent most of her own savings on various expensive treatments and examinations.

'We shall take care of those, Miss Hilton,' Dr. Johansen assured her. 'If necessary, my friend, Mr. Firth, will be able to deduct amounts from your salary when you return,' he added with a twinkle.

Felicity raced home to tell Trevor, but he showed little enthusiasm.

'Another session of doctors probing me about,' he grumbled.

'But, Trevor, such a chance might not come again for both of us,' she pointed out gently.

'All very well for you. You can go about and enjoy yourself.' He walked moodily towards the window. 'Oh, well, if it'll make you happy, I suppose I'm willing. It would be a change, anyway.'

She put her arms round his neck and kissed his cheek.

'Besides,' she added slyly, 'it's an island. Lots of water and opportunities for messing about with boats.'

He released himself abruptly. 'Boats!' he murmured. 'Yes, of course. Well, that makes it almost worth while.'

Trevor had been denied so many opportunities of sport, but more than anything, he loved sailing.

All travelling arrangements were made by Dr. Johansen and Mr. Firth, so Felicity had only to find a suitable sub-tenant for the flat and pack her own and Trevor's clothes.

She could hardly believe that in the space of a week she was leaving behind the familiar and interesting lunch-time view of the Thames from London Bridge, the wharves busy unloading barges, cranes swinging ashore bundles of timber, crates of furs and overhead gulls wheeling and diving. Now she was heading for an island where Dr. Johansen said that as well as cloudless skies and sapphire seas, there were orchards of pomegranate trees.

After the plane journey to Milan, Trevor was bored and restless in the train to Ancona.

'Try to sleep if you can,' his sister urged him, and although she could easily have dozed, too, she fixed her attention on the exciting scenery outside the windows. Hills and valleys and wide green plains, with towns perched on crags or nestling at the foot of a wooded slope. She would probably never have the chance of visiting so much of Italy again and was determined to make the most of it now.

It was not difficult to see that she and Trevor were sister and brother. Trevor's features had not yet blunted into a man's face, but still retained the same fine bone structure as Felicity's. His hair had darkened to a light brown, where hers was a rich red-gold, but their eyes were the same dark blue, an unusual and unfair combination for a redhead, so Felicity had been teased by her friends.

Now as she gazed at her slenderly built brother with his delicate face paled by fatigue, she was filled with compassion tinged with apprehension for his future. If this promised new treatment failed, what then?

Before they left London, Dr. Johansen had met Trevor, promising nothing but an excellent chance of a cure.

'If a cure is at all possible, then I'm sure my friend won't fail,' he had assured the boy.

The steamer from Ancona to Bari did not call at the Lamini islands, but stopped to allow intending passengers to go ashore by launch. It was early evening when Felicity and Trevor landed at the tiny harbour of the largest of the three islands. She had an impression of rocky shores crowned with dense, green vegetation, a cluster of houses climbing the hill.

Dr. Johansen had been compelled by an urgent case to return a day or two earlier. 'Otherwise, I would have

accompanied you and your brother all the way,' he told
Felicity. But he had promised to meet them on arrival and
now she looked for his tall, fair-headed figure.

The rest of the passengers from the launch had all dis-
persed, except for three Italians who remained on the quayside, talking volubly until at last they moved across the
road to a café.

An importunate Italian boy kept nudging Felicity's
elbow. 'You want hotel? I take you,' he promised.

While she was wondering what next to do, a car drew up
and a young man hastily alighted and came towards
Felicity.

'Miss Hilton? And your brother?' he greeted them
breathlessly. 'I'm terribly sorry to be so late, but Dr.
Johansen asked me to meet you both and I was delayed. He
apologises for not meeting you himself, but he was unable
to come. I'm Dr. Bennett, Noel Bennett, one of Dr. Johansen's assistants.'

He attended to the luggage, settled Felicity and Trevor
in the car and drove off up the hill, then between massive
gates and along a drive through extensive and colourful
grounds.

On the way he told her that the clinic had formerly been
a summer residence of an Italian Duke. 'Before that it was
a monastery, and you'll see that the cloisters come in very
handily for our patients.

'I'll take you to the main building first,' he said, 'but
don't get out of the car until I find out where your accommodation is.'

He vanished up some wide marble steps, then beyond a
doorway set in a massive portico.

'H'm. Quite a place,' remarked Trevor.

Noel Bennett was back within a few minutes. 'You're
booked in at one of the villas in the grounds. You'll be
comfortable there because our only English nurse also lives
there. D'you speak Italian?'

'Hardly a word,' confessed Felicity. 'But I intend to
learn.'

10

He conducted her and Trevor into a marble-floored vestibule, then into a large room furnished with easy chairs, sofas and small tables piled with magazines and books.

'Isobel!' he called out, and almost immediately a tall, dark-haired girl dressed in nurse's uniform appeared at the foot of a wide staircase.

'I've brought the new visitors,' he told her, and rapidly introduced Felicity and Trevor to Isobel Claremont.

Felicity's room was delightful, she thought, with cool green and white furnishings and a spacious balcony overlooking the gardens.

'Oh, it's marvellous,' she exclaimed to Nurse Claremont, who had already taken Trevor to his room at the end of the corridor.

'Good. I'm glad you like it,' returned Isobel. 'On the whole our working conditions are excellent here, especially when I remember what it was like working in Birmingham. The hospital was very good, but it took so long to get out of the city into any kind of open country.'

'That applies even more to London,' Felicity commented. 'You spend so much time and money trying to get away from streets.'

'We've come to ridiculous extremes here. Lamini hasn't exactly the gaiety. In fact, it isn't a tourist spot at all—yet, and the mainland is nearly fifteen miles away. Even then, you're more or less in the middle of nowhere.'

'But you like it here?' queried Felicity.

'I'm interested in the work that goes on here, but I don't expect to stay more than a year or two. If you want help with unpacking, I can send a maid,' she added, after a pause.

'Oh no. I'm not used to that sort of luxury.'

'Dinner is in about an hour, so you'll have time for a bath and change. The dining-room is to the right of the staircase.'

Isobel nodded companionably and whisked away in her all-white uniform.

Felicity flung herself into an upholstered armchair. What

a contrast this room with its airy lightness to the dingy little bedroom in the London flat! No shopping on the way home or in snatched minutes at lunch-time, no heating bills to pay, no turning out on a wet or cold morning to jostle with fellow-passengers in the Tube. Oh, this was to be a heavenly few months for her and Trevor as well, and if his sight could be improved and blindness averted, then she would put up with all the dreary inconveniences of working in London again when she and her brother returned.

She strolled out to her balcony, drinking in the wonderful sight, the shrubs with blazing flowers, gaudy yellows and reds, flowers she had never seen before and whose names she did not know. Away on the edge of the grounds tall umbrella pines were sharply silhouetted against the lemon evening sky.

She heard voices below, then a man's laugh. 'Isobel, you're going to have your pretty little nose pushed right out of joint when Burne Mallory sees our new arrival.'

The voice belonged to Noel Bennett who had driven her here.

Felicity took a step towards her room door, feeling that she had no right to listen to a conversation not meant for her, but curiosity overcame her. Who was Burne Mallory and why should Isobel's nose be pushed out of joint? Felicity had no intention of altering the angle of anyone's nose.

Isobel was answering. 'My dear Noel, you jump too fast to conclusions. Actually, I hardly think she's Burne's type.'

Felicity remained stock-still. She could scarcely be sure that she was being discussed. There might have been other new arrivals today.

'What?' exclaimed Noel. 'With that red hair and blue eyes! If I weren't so involved already, I could fall for her myself.'

'Go ahead!' returned Isobel. 'What's to stop you?'

Felicity could not hear Noel's reply and now she walked firmly into her room, refusing to eavesdrop any longer. There was bound to be gossip, she reflected, about every

12

new arrival, whether patient or worker.

When she was dressed in a sleeveless turquoise shift bound at arm-holes and hem with white, she went along to Trevor's room, but apparently he had already gone downstairs.

She saw him ambling about the garden and linked her arm in his.

'D'you like the place?' she asked.

'M'm. So far. Whether I'll go on liking it when I'm having my beastly eyes messed about remains to be seen.'

In the dining-room which was comparatively small, Isobel introduced Felicity and Trevor to the only two other occupants, a couple of Italian nurses, who were already seated at the table.

'You'll understand,' explained Isobel, 'that we have to fit in our meals with our duties sometimes and we can't always wait. Luella and Maria have to be back on duty very soon.'

'Of course. I know that nurses don't keep office hours,' returned Felicity.

Isobel grinned. 'Nor will you when Hendrik gets into his stride again. He'll demand you at all sorts of odd hours.'

'I shan't mind.' Felicity smiled. 'After all, I've come here to work, not to idle all the time.'

'Oh, Hendrik will keep you at it, never fear,' prophesied Isobel.

Dr. Hendrik Johansen came into the dining-room just when Felicity and Trevor had finished their meal.

'I'm full of apologies that I wasn't able to meet you, as I promised, but welcome here all the same. Did you have a good journey?'

'Excellent. Everything according to plan,' replied Felicity.

'I want you to have a couple of days free before we start work,' continued the doctor. 'Laze in the garden or explore the island, just as you choose. This island is not very large, but very beautiful in most parts. Isobel will give you any help you want or information about what there is to do.'

Isobel, who had been standing by the door, laughed. 'Telling Miss Hilton what there is to do here won't take long. One beach fit for bathing, complete with tumbledown shack masquerading as a café, a few shops or stalls along the quay, a couple of cafés and a dancing place of rather dubious character.'

Dr. Johansen raised his fair eyebrows. 'All has become humdrum to you, Isobel, but to Miss Hilton and her brother, it might still be a novelty.'

'There'll be boat trips to the other islands?' queried Felicity hastily.

'Ferry services,' answered the doctor, 'but it's easy enough to get a boatman to take you at any time.'

'Then Trevor and I will be quite happy pottering about among the islands,' she declared with a slight emphasis directed at Isobel, who seemed determined to disparage whatever humble delights the islands might offer. But Isobel Claremont had already disappeared.

'I think an early night would do you both good,' Dr. Johansen advised. 'Travelling to this out-of-the-way place is exhausting.'

When he had bade them both good night, Felicity gave Trevor a questioning glance. 'How d'you feel about an early night? Are you tired? Or shall we walk about for a while?'

'Is it far down to the harbour?' he asked.

'Well, it seemed to take only a few minutes in the car that brought us. We ought to be able to find our way easily enough. I'll get a jacket in case it's chilly later.'

Once outside the gates of the clinic there was a wide view of the sea, and then round a curve of the road the harbour. Although the road was rough for walking, it was downhill.

'Not much of it, anyway,' commented Felicity. 'I expect we could get a taxi back if you're tired later.'

Trevor's interest kindled considerably as he examined with a critical eye the few boats moored or drawn up on the farther side of the harbour.

'I wonder if they ever get any yachts here,' he murmured.

'No doubt some put in occasionally,' Felicity replied. 'And there are sure to be small sailing boats or fishing vessels.'

It was when they were retracing their steps along the quay that Trevor stumbled over a mooring rope tied to a bollard. Felicity's attention which had strayed to the shops and stalls on the other side of the road now returned sharply as she heard Trevor's exclamation.

He picked himself up but staggered a little, and she helped him to a nearby seat. Almost immediately half a dozen men and a couple of women clustered around the boy, chattering in their sonorous voices, no doubt asking what had happened, but Felicity could only shake her head to indicate that she did not understand their questions.

'*Inglese*,' she said desperately.

'*Ah, sì!*' One of the men spoke, then nodded his head comprehendingly, as though being English was sufficient explanation of a young man falling down and sitting there half fainting.

With Felicity on one side and the Italian on the other, they hoisted Trevor to his feet. 'To café! Mariano's,' he shouted, and guided Felicity to the café opposite.

'Cognac, Mariano!' he ordered, taking charge of the patient and seating him at a small table.

Trevor gulped down the brandy and Felicity was relieved to see him recovering quickly.

'Have some yourself,' he invited his sister. 'Good stuff. I feel fine now. I was just knocked out for the moment.'

Felicity took a sip or two of the spirit and felt her own confidence returning. Even a small accident to Trevor made her nervous of the consequences, for he had been told by various specialists that any kind of head injury might hasten his blindness.

Mariano, the café proprietor, stood by the table along with the man who had helped Trevor. Felicity murmured, '*Grazie. Tante grazie.*' At least she could muster enough Italian from the phrase-book to sound both polite and grateful. She put a thousand-lire note on the table and

15

made signs to indicate that both men should have a drink.

The two Italians beamed and smiled at her. Then a tall figure joined the two men. 'Excuse me, but I gather you're English. Can I help you?'

Felicity was so relieved to find someone who apparently was as English as herself that she babbled out the brief story of Trevor's fall.

'Are you staying here?' he asked.

'Yes. At the hospital. Dr. Johansen's clinic.'

His expression changed. She had already received an impression of a tanned face, dark hair, a dominant chin line and a penetrating glance from deep-set grey eyes. Now he seemed both surprised and faintly amused.

'If your brother is fit enough, I'll try to get you the island's only taxi, if the driver can be found. Mariano!' he called to the plump Italian behind the bar, then spoke in rapid Italian.

'Si, signor. Si, si,' replied Mariano, and in turn bawled a message to someone else.

Mariano brought Felicity her change from the note and the Englishman counted it, extracted a few lire which he handed to Mariano.

After a minute or so a battered old car appeared outside the café, and Felicity and Trevor clambered in. Considering the car's ancient exterior, the upholstery inside was surprisingly clean if a trifle shabby.

The young driver, addressed as Tomaso, received his instructions, and after a preliminary session of bangs and snorts the car rattled away. A glance out of the rear window showed Felicity that the tall man was still standing outside Mariano's in the patch of light from the café. Then a bend of the road hid him from view.

The night was quite dark now and away from the concentrated lights near the harbour it was impossible to distinguish sea from sky. A few lights twinkled far away and Felicity supposed they were on one of the other islands.

'The young man is better?' Tomaso asked over his shoulder.

'Yes, I'm all right now,' answered Trevor.

'You speak English well,' commented Felicity to the driver.

'Oh, I work one time on the steamers *Napoli, Sorrento, Capri.* Many English tourists, so I learn. I talk better than Mariano,' he asserted boastfully, negotiating a rough corner with a violent swerve. 'Signor Mallory help me.'

Felicity's interest was immediately aroused. 'Signor Mallory? You know him?'

Tomaso laughed. '*Si signorina.* You also. The Englishman in Mariano's. You talk to him.'

'Oh, I didn't realise—I didn't know his name.'

Tomaso laughed again and swung round in his seat to look at Felicity. 'Signor Mallory always like the pretty girl, yes?'

'I don't know anything about that.' She wished Tomaso would keep his attention on his driving, for the headlights revealed a rough, stony road running between bushes and jutting boulders of rock.

But eventually he swung his ancient car through the hospital gates and stopped outside the main door of the building.

Felicity asked, 'How much?' then ventured, '*Quanto costa?*' Tomaso shook his head. 'Signor Mallory has paid me, *signorina. Buona sera.*'

'Who's this Mallory chap?' asked Trevor as he and his sister walked towards the villa where they were staying.

'Someone who lives here or has stayed on the island for some time. Anyway, I was very glad he was able to help us down there by the harbour.'

When she had assured herself that Trevor was comfortably settled in bed and appeared to be no worse for tripping over a rope, she returned to her own room, still wondering what connection, if any, the man called Burne Mallory had with the clinic. That fragment of overheard conversation earlier today repeated itself in her mind—'*hardly Burne's type*'. Well, from what she had seen of him, he was hardly her type, she told herself, although, of course, he had been

17

helpful in Mariano's café. She must remember if she met him again that she owed him a taxi fare.

The next day Dr. Hendrik Johansen spent a large part of his day in escorting Felicity and Trevor to various parts of the island.

From the top of the hill behind the clinic it was possible to see the mainland, a blurred smudge on the horizon.

'Also the other two Lamini islands,' explained Dr. Hendrik. 'That one is Isola Rondine—that means "swallow". The very small one there is named Isola Lupa, for some say it is the shape of a wolf.'

'What about this one?' asked Felicity. 'Is it just Lamini?'

'No, this is Isola Rossa. The Red Island. The legend is that in the time of smugglers and pirates, the island appeared red because of the pomegranate flowers in summer.'

'I've never seen pomegranates in flower,' she murmured.

'Then you'll have opportunities here. Next month, June, all the orchards will glow with flame flowers.'

'When am I going to be examined?' broke in Trevor harshly.

Felicity turned towards him in surprise. Usually Trevor was anxious to postpone examinations and new treatments and she had imagined that he would enjoy this small preliminary period of leisure as much as she.

'In a day or so,' answered Dr. Johansen. 'There are a few preparations to be made first.'

In the evening when Dr. Johansen had left Felicity and Trevor in the hall of their villa, Trevor said, 'Let's go out sailing tomorrow. Otherwise, I can see I'm not going to have the chance afterwards for a while.'

'Well, I don't know if we can make plans like that,' she said dubiously. 'The doctor might want to make arrangements for us.'

'What if he does? If you're going to work for him as his secretary, you don't have to kow-tow to him the whole of the twenty-four hours. Besides, he definitely told us that we could have a couple of days to ourselves and do what we

18

liked.'

'You sounded over-anxious to start treatment straight-away,' she reminded him.

'Certainly I did not. I just wanted to know so that I wasn't pounced on just when I'd decided to do something I liked.'

'All right,' agreed Felicity. 'We'll see if a boat is available tomorrow. Probably we can ask Dr. Johansen.'

'For pity's sake! D'you want him to hold your hand all the time? If you do that, ten chances to one he'll want to come along with us.'

'He'll probably be too busy to spare the time to play around with us,' retorted Felicity. 'And if he did come, where would be the harm in that? He knows the waters round the islands better than you do.'

Trevor frowned. 'Stop fussing, Flissie dear, or you'll be an old woman before your time.'

Felicity laughed. Her brother knew that he had only to use that old pet name and a gentle, amiable tone of voice for her to fall in with his plans.

When she and Trevor went down to the harbour next morning, she thought it prudent first to ask Mariano at the café what should be the average price for a few hours' sailing.

'Ah, it is good to see you both so well.' Then he pursed his lips, named a figure in lire and pointed out a slim, dark-haired lad idling on the quay.

'He has a boat. Ask him. His name is Fortunato, but everyone call him Forto.'

After a little haggling, Trevor had hired the small sailing dinghy for the day and he and Felicity set off towards Isola Rondine.

'I think you'd have done better this first time to allow Forto to come with us,' Felicity suggested when Trevor let the boat heel over at a rather alarming angle. 'He could have told us about the landing places or what to avoid.'

'Nonsense! Look, she's going like a bird now. Don't worry, I shan't capsize.'

19

'I hope not! I'm unprepared to swim long-distance between the islands.'

At Isola Rondine there was an easy stretch of sand where the boat had only to be run ashore. A beach café sold fruit and cheese and little sticky cakes, as well as soft drinks and local wine.

'There you are, you see,' Trevor pointed out, when they had finished their picnic meal on the beach, 'you wouldn't have even met this delightful spot if I hadn't brought you.'

'All right. You can take all the credit,' Felicity answered, only too pleased to see her brother enjoying himself for a few days before the ordeal in store for him.

They lazed for a while in the sun, and later bathed in the warm, gently lapping water. Farther out from the shore, where the strip of sand joined a seabed of rounded pebbles, it was possible to see clearly every stone, every moving shadow from the rippling surface of the water.

Looking back at the shore as she swam parallel, Felicity agreed with her brother that this was indeed a delightful spot, a crescent of pale sand fringed at either end with bushes and pine trees, backed by sloping green-clad hills and above, a cloudless sapphire sky.

'A good idea of yours, Flissie,' remarked Trevor as he lay on the warm sand after his bathe. 'Coming here, I mean. How long did you say this doctor wants you here?'

'I'm not sure. A few months.' Felicity was deliberately vague, for she knew that her term might depend on the progress Trevor made.

'Why did he want someone like you from England?' he asked, rolling over to look at her. 'Should have thought he could have found someone nearer than London who could type English for him.'

'I expect he could. But he just happens to be a friend of Mr. Firth's.'

'H'm. Wonder why his previous girl left him. D'you know?'

'Of course,' returned Felicity. 'She went back to England

to get married.'

The return journey was slow, for there was so little wind that they were almost becalmed.

'We'd better use the oars,' suggested Felicity. 'I'll row and you steer.'

Perversely, a fresh wind sprang up when they neared the harbour of Isola Rossa and Felicity had already shipped the oars when the little dinghy ran towards the quay. More boats were moored there and as Trevor tried to haul down the sail and avoid ramming another boat at the same time, he drifted rapidly towards a smartly painted cabin-cruiser.

'Look out, Trevor!' Felicity called sharply, and seized an oar to fend off, but her warning was too late. Trevor's dinghy hit the motor-cruiser with a sharp crack. Then as he tried to sheer away, he knocked a canoe in which a man was standing. Taken off balance, the man toppled overboard and his canoe capsized after him.

Felicity gave a startled cry and held out an oar for the man to grab, but he was more concerned in righting his canoe. When he clambered in, he shouted a torrent of rapid Italian at Trevor, shaking his fists in threatening gestures.

'Sorry, old chap,' called Trevor apologetically. 'I didn't mean to shoot you overboard.'

Felicity manoeuvred the dinghy close to one of the flight of steps cut in the harbour wall, stepped nimbly ashore to fasten the mooring rope, but found it taken out of her hands as someone went up the steps to the top.

'Thanks very much!' called Trevor to the unseen helper, now out of Felicity's view.

She gathered her bathing things and other belongings and climbed the steps to find Mr. Mallory waiting there.

'Oh, good evening.' She was embarrassed by the know-ledge that he must have witnessed Trevor's difficulties.

Trevor joined her a moment later. 'Thanks for tying up,' he said. 'I suppose you saw that I tipped someone into the water. Bad luck, really. It wouldn't have happened if that tycoon's glossy job hadn't been stuck in the way.'

'Really? Perhaps you ought to find out the owner of the

21

glossy job you cannoned into.'

'Well, naturally, I intend to,' replied Trevor, reddening uncomfortably. 'I suppose you don't happen to know who he is?'

Mr. Mallory smiled, but not pleasantly. 'Look no further. The boat happens to be mine.'

Felicity gasped. 'Oh, Mr. Mallory, we're terribly sorry!'

'I do sincerely apologise,' broke in Trevor. 'I'll pay for any damage.'

Felicity glared at her brother. How could he possibly pay if Mr. Mallory insisted on compensation? He wasn't insured against such a risk and he certainly had no funds of his own.

All the same she said emphatically, 'My brother will certainly pay. It was pure accident.'

'Could happen to anyone,' added Trevor.

Mr. Mallory looked from one to the other and now he seemed amused. 'Then it's lucky it happened to my boat instead of a local fishing boat, or you'd be charged with compensation for lost catches. Here's the man you pushed overboard. I think you'll find he'll accept a thousand-lire note. That'll buy him enough brandy to keep the cold out.'

She took the note from her bag and handed it to Trevor, then turned back to Mr. Mallory. 'You'd better know our names,' she said coldly. 'It's Hilton. Felicity and Trevor. You know where we're staying, so please send the bill to me. I'll also add last night's taxi fare. Good night, Mr. Mallory.'

She walked away with all the dignity she could muster; wearing shorts and a blue shirt-top and sandals are not the most successful garments for parading one's displeasure, but she hoped that Mr. Mallory would notice that she was not amused by his high-handed attitude.

When she realised that Trevor was not with her, she turned and called to him. He was still talking to Mr. Mallory, who grinned and apparently told Trevor to hurry along.

Trevor caught her up. 'Why the hurry? I might have

22

made a good contact there. That boat of his happens to be the best in the harbour.'

'And you had to damage it!' snapped Felicity crossly.

'Oh, not much. Paint scratched a bit, probably. Nothing to worry about, and Mallory was quite decent about the whole thing. I'd give a lot to go out in his boat.'

'We've already received enough favours from him without cadging boat trips.'

Trevor laughed. 'Why are you so piqued about the man?'

'I'm not at all piqued,' she retorted. 'I just think it's far too soon for us to involve ourselves with people here. We know nothing about Mr. Mallory except that he happens to be English——'

'And has a marvellous boat,' finished Trevor.

'In that case, for all we know, he's just cruising and only staying here for a short time.'

Felicity was glad when Dr. Johansen suggested that evening that she might like to start work next day.

'I thought you could get a general idea of what is involved if you looked through some of the files and correspondence. I shan't demand that you start slaving straightaway.'

She spent the morning as he instructed and found that much of the work concerned reports on various case histories of patients, keeping record cards up to date and so on. Dr. Johansen had already explained to her before she accepted the post that he would not require much technical or medical knowledge on her part.

She was slightly worried about Trevor and warned him not to go sailing alone. She knew, even if he did not, that his defective eyesight might land him in further trouble.

But at dinner he assured her that he had spent the day in a manner with which she could hardly find fault.

'I went down to the harbour, then round that little point. There's quite a good bathing beach there. When I came back, I stopped in Mariano's café for an hour or so.'

She smiled at her brother. 'Good. I'm glad you kept out

of mischief. Have you enough pocket money for the time being?' She knew how much Trevor hated asking her for small amounts of personal money.

'I'm O.K. Odds and ends don't cost much here, apparently.'

Towards the end of the following day Dr. Johansen told Felicity that Trevor was to have his preliminary examination next day.

'Nothing very drastic,' he assured her. 'About ten o'clock. One of the nurses will take you to the eye clinic and I've arranged that you can be present on this first occasion, although that may not be possible at future times.'

'I understand,' returned Felicity. 'I'll see that Trevor is warned.'

'Right. Let's get the thing over,' was Trevor's comment when she told him. Considering all the various treatments he had been subjected to over the past two years, she thought he was reasonably philosophical about his future. 'If this quack can really do something for me, then I'll be able to go in for all kinds of sport.'

A nurse conducted Felicity and Trevor into a waiting-room at the eye clinic, which was a separate building in the grounds. After a few moments the young Italian girl called them into the consulting-room.

A white-coated figure was standing at a filing cabinet. He turned and said, 'Sit down, both of you.'

'Mr. Mallory!' Felicity gasped.

Trevor merely looked surprised and said, 'Well, well! Who'd have thought you were going to be my next quack?'

'You both seem astonished at my profession,' Mr. Mallory said. 'Did you think I was just a loafer?'

'No—but I didn't know you worked here,' stammered Felicity.

'Then allow me to present myself. Burne Mallory, with a few qualifying letters after my name.'

'What I meant was that Dr. Johansen didn't mention that the specialist Trevor was to see was English.'

Burne Mallory raised his dark eyebrows. 'Is that counted

24

against me? You'd rather have another nationality? Swiss, perhaps? I know many distinguished Swiss colleagues in my line. Or Swedish, like Johansen?'

Felicity reddened with embarrassment and resentment. Between them, she and Trevor had not made a happy start to an association from which they both hoped to gain so much.

'Shall we begin the examination, Miss Hilton, with your permission?'

On Dr. Johansen's advice, Felicity had brought with her such notes as she had on Trevor's condition and she asked diffidently if Mr. Mallory would like to see them first.

'Not at present,' he replied. 'I prefer to make a first diagnosis on my own.'

She was glad when the examination was over, but she did not ask Mr. Mallory for his opinion about a cure. Even in that she managed to appear in the wrong, for as she and Trevor prepared to leave the consulting-room, Mr. Mallory queried, 'Don't you want to know what sort of hope I might offer?'

She looked at him and refused to flinch from the challenge in his grey eyes. 'I know better than to ask specialists for snap decisions, Mr. Mallory,' she said coolly. 'Nor would it be kind to my brother either to raise his hopes or cast him down by bad news. No doubt you will let us know if you're prepared to give him any kind of treatment.'

'I assure you that I shan't neglect an interesting case.' She saw the veiled irony in his face and was glad that Trevor had already gone out of the room ahead.

'An interesting case,' she repeated quietly. 'I understand quite well that he's no more than that to you, but more important to me.'

'Naturally, I, too, understand that you're emotionally involved. I'll see him again in a couple of days. In the meantime, insist that he wears his dark glasses all the time, especially out of doors. The sunlight is strong here.'

Felicity nodded her compliance. 'Thank you, Mr. Mallory.'

When she rejoined Trevor, she found him in a black, despondent mood.

'An interesting case!' he mocked. 'Oh, I heard! That's what they all say, but they don't find out the trouble or do anything to cure it.'

'Perhaps this is the one chance in a million,' she tried to assure him, 'and Mr. Mallory will find a cure.'

CHAPTER TWO

LATER that day Noel Bennett came to the villa and suggested that she might like to go dancing with him and a few others tonight.

'I'd like to,' replied Felicity, 'but could I bring Trevor as well? I can't leave him at a loose end.'

'Sure. I'll fix him up with a partner or two when we get there.'

'Thank you, Dr. Bennett.'

'Oh, not so formal, please. My name's Noel. We drop all our starchiness in a place like this. Even Johansen is usually known as Hendrik.'

Trevor brightened up at the prospect of dancing. 'It'll pass the time,' he murmured. He cheered up still more when he found that Noel's other passenger besides Felicity was Luella, one of the two Italian nurses who took their meals in the villa.

'Isobel was coming, too,' explained Noel, 'but she had to take an emergency duty.'

The café to which he drove was on the other side of the harbour and the floor only a small cleared space between the bar and a single row of tables lining the wall.

'A bit congested here,' Noel explained, when the music suddenly blared out of a radiogram behind the bar. 'But usually good fun, and in a place like Rossa, we can't be too choosy.'

Felicity was aware of the interested glances from dark-eyed Italian girls and the openly sensual admiration from their partners. She tried not to notice when the men deliberately jostled her as she danced with Noel, who was an energetic performer. In a short time her strength was used up and she confessed that she'd have to sit out a tune or two.

27

'Outside then,' suggested Noel. 'Much cooler and more pleasant than in here.'

Across the road was a rounded piece of harbour wall and here there were tables under trees from which festoons of coloured lights were suspended.

Noel ordered some wine and poured a generous measure into Felicity's glass.

'Here's to us!' he exclaimed. 'And devil take the future!' he added recklessly.

'Why d'you say that?' she asked.

He shrugged. 'Heaven knows. I wish I could make up my mind.'

'About your future?'

'Yes. That and other things.'

'How long have you been here? With Dr. Johansen, I mean.'

'Just over a year. I came at his invitation. Otherwise I would never have heard of the place. He specialises in chest diseases, but I expect you know that.'

'No, I didn't know,' admitted Felicity. 'At least, not until I started working on his reports and case histories.'

'As that's also my own line, I thought the experience of working with him would be valuable when I went back to England. But now—well, I don't know. I'm not sure that I want to go back. You see, Felicity—you don't mind if I call you that, do you?'

'Of course not. Go ahead.'

But before he could utter another word, two people passed their table and one of them stopped abruptly.

Noel looked up. 'Oh, it's you, Mallory!'

In the fitful glitter of the fairy-lights, Mr. Mallory's face appeared harsh, even saturnine.

'I suppose I'd better introduce you.' He turned towards Felicity. 'This is Burne Mallory——'

'We've already met,' interrupted Mr. Mallory.

'Oh, trust you not to lose time!' growled Noel.

'Actually, on two levels, if I may say so. The purely personal—although accidental—and the professional. Miss

28

Hilton's brother is about to become a patient of mine.'

Felicity noticed that Isobel Claremont had slipped ahead of Mr. Mallory and seated herself at another table, thus making it quite plain that she did not want her partner, Mr. Mallory, to join Noel and Felicity.

Isobel's voice called sweetly, 'Burne!' In a moment or two Burne Mallory obeyed the summons. When he had gone out of earshot, Noel said savagely, 'Now I see why Isobel had an unexpected "emergency" duty. She'd better look out for herself, though. Mallory picks up girls by the dozen and when he's tired of them—bang! Dropped like a hot potato.'

Felicity smiled gently. 'If he's like that, then I'm surprised he's come to such a remote place as this.'

'Oh, it's rumoured that he came here to hide. A scandal blew up in London and he vanished. Successful eye specialists don't choose a tiny island like this when they could be earning pots of money in London or New York.'

'Perhaps Mr. Mallory prefers the simpler life for a while,' suggested Felicity.

Noel leaned his arms across the table. 'Now don't you go falling for him. Remember I've warned you. He's nothing but the worst kind of playboy. That's what happened to your predecessor, Jill.'

Noel paused to empty his glass and refill it.

'Oh? What happened?'

'There she was working happily for Hendrik when along comes Mallory and immediately she went right overboard for him. Oh, he encouraged her, of course, and she believed every word he said, even believed that he would marry her.'

'And then?' prompted Felicity.

'She was stupid enough to tell everyone that she and Burne were engaged, and when he heard that, he almost threw her in the sea.'

'How d'you know all this, Noel?'

'You think I'm exaggerating, don't you?' He gave her a questioning glance. 'Of course I don't know the half of it, but Jill came to me and poured out the whole story. I tried to calm her down, get her to look sensibly at the whole affair and write it off as a chunk of experience. In the end, she went back to England. She said she'd had enough and couldn't stay here. If she did, she'd probably take an overdose of something or drive a car over the edge of the cliff. So she went back to England.'

'But I thought she went back to get married. Dr. Johansen told me——'

'Hendrik was so furious at losing his good secretary that he covered up for Jill the best way he could. In fact, I suspect that he was a little bit smitten himself with Jill. She was very pretty and full of fun. Hendrik and Burne haven't been quite the same with each other since she went. Oh, I know that professionally they're on excellent terms, but Hendrik has a few personal reservations, I'm quite sure, and no wonder.'

If Felicity had known Noel rather longer, she would have pointed out that his disparagement of Burne Mallory was caused less by Jill's sufferings than his own where Isobel was concerned. Noel's jealousy was plain enough and undoubtedly he was sore because for the moment, anyway, Isobel preferred Burne.

It occurred to Felicity that Noel might have ideas about using her as a counter-attraction to win back Isobel through jealousy. Or was it possible that by blackening Burne's reputation so thoroughly, Noel hoped that Felicity, too, would enter the lists and compete for Burne, ousting Isobel so that he would have only to hold out his arms for Isobel's return?

All these thoughts ran through Felicity's mind as she sat with Noel, sipping the rough, heady wine, and guiding the conversation into different channels. She hadn't known Noel long enough to try to give him advice, or bring out into the open what she suspected.

She was determined, however, that she was here to work for Hendrik Johansen and she would certainly keep out of the way of Burne Mallory, whether he was the breaker of hearts that Noel declared or merely an attractive magnet towards which girls were powerless to prevent themselves drifting.

She was sure that Burne knew what he wanted from life and would accept it only on his own terms or not at all. Naturally she would have to meet him on the professional level in connection with Trevor's treatment, but there need be nothing more personal than that. Nothing must jeopardise Trevor's chance of success in defeating approaching blindness.

Trevor himself had been well pleased to spend the evening with Luella, and when Felicity decided it was time to go home, she had to run the pair to earth in a very dark corner of the harbour café.

'Ready to go home?' she said, pretending not to notice that Trevor's arm was tightly wound around Luella's trim waist.

'Good heavens! So soon?' he complained.

But Luella composedly withdrew from Trevor's clasp. 'Yes. It is time. I have to be on duty at seven o'clock to-morrow morning.'

In the back of the car on the way home, Felicity could hear Luella patiently giving Trevor lessons in Italian. As long as the education stopped at languages, Felicity was content, for she did not want complications with Trevor becoming infatuated with pretty Italian girls.

Felicity's work for Dr. Hendrik Johansen absorbed her completely for the next two days. There were several piles of reports to be typed not only in English but also in German and Italian. She was glad that as copy typist she had the facility of visualising words in a foreign language although she did not necessarily understand the meaning. In London she had often worked on Swedish and Norwegian documents.

At the same time a thin thread of wonder penetrated her absorption. After the unhappy experience of his previous English secretary, she was surprised that Dr. Hendrik had gone to some lengths to engage another English girl. True, most of the correspondence was in English, for he communicated chiefly with London, Washington, New York and Montreal. When he wanted letters in Italian, he dictated them to a tape-recorder and the correspondence was typed by an Italian assistant.

'Your brother has been examined again this afternoon by Mr. Mallory,' the doctor told her when he came into her office. 'There is nothing definite yet.'

'You mean he hasn't yet found the cause?' she asked.

Dr. Johansen nodded. 'It takes time, you understand, and Mr. Mallory has his own excellent methods.'

'I offered Mr. Mallory all the notes I had of previous treatments, but——'

Dr. Johansen smiled as he interrupted her. 'I know, but a new treatment must start completely unbiased by what has gone before. That is the secret of a fresh mind approaching the problem.'

'Yes, of course, and I'll try to be patient and not expect results too soon.'

She was finding it very pleasant to work for Dr. Johansen. While, as Isobel had prophesied, he did not keep to a rigid five-day week with fixed hours, he was generous with free time when the work allowed.

One morning about eleven o'clock he said, 'There's nothing very urgent for the rest of the day. Take some time off and enjoy yourself.'

'Thank you.'

A few moments before, Burne Mallory had come into Dr. Johansen's office and the two men discussed a particular case.

Felicity finished the report she had been typing and left the two men together, but she had taken only a few steps along the corridor when Burne Mallory came striding behind her.

'Miss Hilton! Would you like to spend some of your free afternoon with me?'

She was caught unawares by his offer and hesitated.

He grinned. 'I was in Hendrik's office, so you can't plead

you're in a rush of work. But perhaps you were going to wash your hair or something?'

His needling remark had given her time to compose herself.

'I was thinking more of Trevor,' she said. 'He doesn't go out often unless I'm with him.'

He looked at her with raised eyebrows that might have meant disbelief of one or both her statements.

'Your brother will be very happy and comfortable for the rest of the day. He is in my clinic, with music to listen to if he wants it and a very pretty nurse to look at and talk to.'

When she still made no reply, he continued, 'If you've no further objections to my company, I'd like to talk to you— about your brother.'

Felicity smiled up at him. Was he using an unfair tactic, knowing that she would agree if he mentioned Trevor's welfare? She could not be sure.

'Yes, of course I'll come. I'll be glad to.'

His face crinkled into a smile. 'I'll give you fifteen minutes, no more, and I'll be at the main entrance.'

With the curtest of nods he went off in the opposite direction, leaving Felicity with the feeling that she hadn't put up much of a fight. That was her first reaction. Then it dawned on her that to put up a fight at all with Burne Mallory was merely to invite him to a trial of strength. That was the way no doubt many other girls had started, only to find themselves longing for his invitations. She would not fall into that trap. No, quite the best way was to comply in a friendly way as if he were a grey-haired old gentleman who was Trevor's specialist.

As she hurried towards her villa, the idea of Burne Mallory ever being a benign, grey-haired old gentleman made her laugh. Grey hair might come with the ravages of time, but benign he never would be.

She was about to change her dress for something more casual, but decided not to give Burne the impression that she was dressing for his benefit.

When she arrived at the main entrance he was already

there on the top step and he came quickly down to her level.

'You didn't repent, then?' he asked.

'No. I saw no reason for that.'

They walked towards his car and as she entered, Noel Bennett came round a corner of the main block.

'Hallo, Felicity!' he called, but did not wait for her answering greeting.

Burne drove down the rough road towards the harbour, then stopped. 'We can take my boat and go to Lupa or Rondine as we fancy.'

Her face must have expressed blank surprise. 'What's the matter?' he demanded. 'What are you thinking? "Once aboard the lugger and the girl is mine"?'

She stepped out of the car. 'No. I was thinking how much Trevor would have enjoyed a trip in your boat. He never stops talking about it and he'll be furious if he thinks I've scored over him and gone first.'

'Well, he hasn't lost the chance.' Burne Mallory's face was amused. 'As long as he doesn't want to take charge and steer the ship into a wreck or a pile of rocks.'

The smart motor-cruiser rose and fell indolently on the water at the foot of the steps and Burne held the stern steady while Felicity stepped over the side. She saw now that the boat was named *La Perla*.

'The Pearl?' she queried, as he cast off.

'Yes,' he agreed. 'But she's had several other names before that.'

'Did you change her name?'

He nodded. He started the engine with a roar, then throttled down and turned towards her, his lean face sharply lit and shadowed by the sun. 'Before I owned her, she was *Bernardina* but it's a mistake to name a boat after the girl of the moment. It's like having the wrong name tattooed on your chest.'

Felicity laughed at that. 'It makes a job for someone all the same, painting out the old name and putting on the new one. On boats, I mean, not chests.' She laughed again.

34

He regarded her with some intentness. 'D'you know, I'm positive that's the first time I've ever heard you laugh, Miss Sobersides. Really laugh, I mean. You should do it more often. It becomes you.'

'Laughing usually becomes everyone—if they have anything to laugh about,' she returned quietly.

'And you? You haven't had much happiness? Is that what you mean?'

Her eyes must have momentarily clouded, for she had a blurred vision of Philip's face when he had said his final goodbye.

'Oh, as much as most people,' she managed to say calmly.

'Tell me about your parents—unless that distresses you.'

'No, not now. I expect you know the facts already. My parents were killed in an avalanche disaster in Austria. That was six years ago, when I was eighteen and Trevor was only twelve.'

'Who took care of you both?' he queried.

'No one. Trevor was at boarding-school and sometimes good holidays could be arranged for him with other boys or with school parties. I had just finished my secretarial training, so I took a few temporary jobs at first to get experience. Then I looked for something more permanent. Something with enough salary for me to pay a share of a flat with a couple of other girls.'

'But you must have had some relatives. Why didn't you live with them?'

Felicity laughed quietly. 'There was an aunt and uncle with a host of cousins. They have a farm in the north of Scotland. My mother has two sisters, one widowed and the other an invalid. They live near Sidmouth and lead a very quiet life. You couldn't expect them to disrupt their lives for the sake of one boisterous schoolboy and one not-very-clever girl just starting to earn a living.'

'So you took the hard way and preferred your independence?'

'If you see it that way, yes,' she answered. 'We had a

35

house in Norwood, rather large and old-fashioned, and as the lease had nearly run out, the solicitors advised me to sell. It was either that or modernise the place and let it in flats. I didn't really fancy myself as a landlady.'

He gave her his quick smile. 'Why not? Although you'd have made a very bad landlady, I think.'

'Why?'

'Too soft. Too generous. You'd have let the tenants walk over you.'

'I wouldn't. I'd have been very strict,' she protested, then subsided into a little giggle. 'Well, no, perhaps I wouldn't. I'd have wanted people to be comfortable.'

'You'd have let them off their rent when they were hard up, and that's very bad for their morale. That's how folks get into debt.' He gave her a severe, scolding look.

She stared at him. 'Well, I didn't do any of these things, so I'm not to blame.'

He turned the boat into a wide circle as they were now approaching the island. 'What was your father? His profession, I mean.'

If she thought Mr. Mallory unduly inquisitive, she did not resent his questions. She had answered similar enquiries from several previous eye specialists.

'He did research work in chemistry. He had just been given charge of a new technical laboratory when he and my mother went to Austria for that holiday. They were celebrating the reward for many years of hard work.'

'Did he have any kind of eye trouble, do you know?'

Felicity frowned for an instant. All these details were included in the notes which Mr. Mallory had refused to accept. 'None at all, except that he wore spectacles for certain kinds of work. So do many other people.'

'Of course. Trevor says it's about three years ago when his sight began to give trouble. That right?'

'Yes, about that.'

'Nothing to account for it? No blow on the head, for instance? What sports did he go in for? Boxing, diving, horse riding?'

'Certainly not boxing. He swims, but he's not an expert diver and, I'm afraid,' she added with a smile, 'there wasn't much money to spare for riding.'

The boat had arrived at Isola Rondine, but not at the same point where she and Trevor had landed on a previous occasion. Here they were close to a rocky wall and Burne threw out three rubber tyre fenders over the side of his boat to keep her off. He moored to the bottom rungs of an iron ladder and held the boat steady.

'Can you manage this?' he asked.

She gave him a straight look. 'Isn't it rather late in the day to ask me that? How d'you know if I've a head for heights or climbing wall ladders?'

'I took a chance on it. Up you go!' He began to chuckle. 'You really do reprove me, don't you? I'll guarantee to catch you if you fall.'

She swung herself on to the ladder and climbed up hand over hand without difficulty. At the top she remembered that she had left her handbag on the boat and she called down to tell him.

'I'm bringing it in my teeth!' he shouted.

'Good old Rover!' she muttered. 'Good dog!'

She had not realised that the clear air would carry her remark down to him. When he joined her on the stone-paved patch at the top, he said, 'Don't ever believe that I'm the type to fetch and carry.'

'No, I won't. I'm sorry you heard what I said.'

'That means you're not sorry you linked me with a pet retriever?'

'Argue if you like, Mr. Mallory. I'll admit straightaway that I'm beaten.'

'Argue? You're an impossible girl to argue with!' he exclaimed. 'Let's have some lunch.'

She had been only once before to this island and on that occasion she and Trevor had spent most of their time in the little bathing cove. Now she could see that this part of Isola Rondine was higher, with a rugged coastline and clumps of dense bushes.

'Is there a village here?' she asked.

'A very small one. A church, a few houses and shops. We're not going there yet.'

He led her down a slope to a sandy patch and to a house almost surrounded by bushes, oleanders, yuccas and hydrangeas. Chickens squawked and flew across the small courtyard, a black and white cat stretched itself lazily, regarded the visitors with bland unconcern, then curled itself into a ball again in the shade of a lemon tree.

He banged on the open door of the house and entered the passage, beckoning to Felicity to follow him.

In a moment a short, plump Italian woman appeared and her face widened into a welcoming smile.

'*Signore!*' she cried, holding out her arms as though to embrace him. '*Veramente!*'

From the confused torrent of Italian that followed, Felicity gathered that first Burne was enquiring after the woman's family, then asking if she could provide lunch for two.

'*Si, si, si!*' came the reply, with much nodding. Felicity was introduced to Signora Lombardo and did not fail to notice the acute look of interest in the woman's glittering black eyes.

She and Burne were conducted towards the shade of a large cedar tree, a table was speedily set and in a few minutes, Felicity was tasting a delicious soup.

'She's an old friend of yours, I take it?' queried Felicity to Burne.

'M'm,' he muttered non-committally. 'When I visit the island she's insulted if I don't visit her.'

The soup was followed by *pizza*, then cheese and fruit, and the whole accompanied by a jug of red wine of some potency.

When they had finished the meal Signora Lombardo joined them in a glass of wine. Evidently Burne's Italian was equal to this rapid conversation, but after a few moments he turned to Felicity and said, 'Forgive us if we talk in Italian. The Signora doesn't understand a word of Eng-

38

lish.' He looked wickedly at his hostess. 'She is a very ugly old woman!' he said slowly.

'No, no!' she exclaimed. *'Non è vero.'* Then she burst into a peal of delighted laughter, her plump shoulders shaking.

'Ah! So you do understand!' he teased her. 'All right. You are not *very* ugly and not *very* old.' Plainly Signora Lombardo did not catch this sarcastic import, for she was as pleased as if he had paid her a great compliment.

Felicity wondered a little if Burne Mallory were trying to show off his powers of attraction over all women, young or old, English or foreign. Then she suppressed such an unworthy thought, for it was not compatible with the pleasant dream-like feeling induced by a good lunch.

In due course, Burne rose when he had finished his cigar, and amid a flurry of thanks and good wishes, he and Felicity finally called *'Arrivederci'* and set out again for another part of the island. She noticed that he had given the Signora a present of some sort and not money to pay for the lunch, so he evidently knew how to be tactful.

A short walk brought them to a small cove, different from the one she and Trevor had found. Although there was a little sand, most of the shore was covered with rocks, a menacing barrier to boats. She must remember to warn Trevor of the hazards on this side of the island.

The path to the beach was narrow and steep and Burne stepped aside when someone was coming up. A girl with thick black hair curling over her shoulders gave him a polite *'Grazie'*, then stared at him with surprise, almost an expression of terror in her dark eyes.

'Hallo, Emilia!' he exclaimed, with apparent delight. Then, in Italian, he was asking how she was and she replied that her family were well. She turned to look at Felicity, giving her an expressionless smile, then her eyes swerved back to Burne and, it seemed to Felicity, the girl quite pointedly fingered the wedding ring on her left hand.

Burne, completely at ease, followed her small, nervous movements, and murmured his congratulations and good wishes. She cast an apprehensive glance towards the beach from which she had come, clutched her white handbag more firmly and turned to go.

'*Addio*,' she said, and Burne replied decisively, '*Arrivederci!*' Felicity knew the difference between the two expressions. '*Addio*' meant a final goodbye. '*Arrivederci*' was the equivalent of '*Au revoir*' and there was something desperate in the girl's face, as though she were trying to say a very final goodbye to Burne.

With a fleeting smile to Felicity, the girl Emilia almost ran up the path and out of sight. A moment or two later, an exceptionally burly Italian with massive shoulders and deep-tanned face came up from the beach, nodded pleasantly to Felicity, but gave Burne a second glance in which uncertainty was mingled with hostility. After a barely perceptible pause he walked on, calling, 'Emilia!'

Felicity and Burne resumed their downward climb in silence.

'Why don't you ask me who that luscious Italian beauty was?' He spoke lightly, but she heard the undercurrent of sarcasm in his voice.

'It's not my business to ask,' she replied calmly. 'You don't have to identify your friends for my benefit.'

'In that case, I'm not going to be denied the opportunity of telling you. Emilia and I had a very heady love affair soon after I came here, but of course it didn't last. Now she's married, so Signora Lombardo told me, and evidently that unpleasant-looking hulk is Carlo, her husband.'

'Are you sorry she's married someone else?'

'Certainly not. Why should I be? I'm not the marrying kind myself, so I don't grudge the girls taking their chance.'

'That's magnanimous of you,' she commented with an upward grin, but she was immediately disconcerted by his unsmiling face, and looked quickly away.

Then he sighed mockingly. 'I don't quite know how to take you, Felicity. I'm damned if I'm going to keep "Miss Hilton-ing" you.'

'That's all right. But you don't have to take me any way.

I just happen to be the sister of one of your patients and I'm working here for a time.'

By now they had arrived at a sandy cove backed by rocks and Felicity's feet sank almost ankle deep in the sand. Fortunately it was only a short distance to a corner shaded by a small pine tree maintaining a precarious hold in the sparse soil.

Burne stretched himself out full length and lit a cigar.

After a prolonged silence he said suddenly, 'What are you running away from? Or is it who?'

She was sitting beside him hugging her knees and gazing towards the dark blue sea. 'What gives you that impression?' she countered.

He grunted. 'Few people would willingly exile themselves to this neck of the woods unless they had several good reasons.'

'That's easy enough. I have—or rather, between us, Trevor and I have several good reasons for coming here. That must be obvious to you.'

'Oh, granted that you brought Trevor here for treatment, yes, that's one excellent reason. But to stay? Was there nothing—or no one—at home who was a counter attraction, even allowing for your devotion to your brother?'

'You're fishing!' she accused him without heat. 'You want to know if there's a man I've left behind me.'

'And is there?' he persisted.

She kept her eyes on the horizon. 'Shall we say—there was?'

He sat up and looked at her. When she turned she saw the sharp planes of his face lit and shadowed by the sunlight, even the dark Latin-type of his features, except that his eyes were dark grey. 'That's better. Tell Uncle all about it.'

She spluttered with laughter, remembering her plan to visualise him as a paternal old greybeard, but she could not tell him that.

'All right,' she agreed. 'We were unofficially engaged, I suppose you could say, but he became tired of waiting.'

'Why did you keep him waiting?' Burne asked.

When she did not answer, he suggested, 'Either you weren't sure you wanted to marry him or else you had crazy notions about noble sacrifices for Trevor's sake.'

That last remark angered her. 'Noble sacrifices don't come into it. While Trevor needs me I'm not going to desert him.'

'Has it ever occurred to you that you're using Trevor as a shield? When you can't make up your mind about something, you fall back on the fact that your brother needs you. What'll you do if his eye trouble is cured? Equally, what are your plans if he really does go blind?'

She gasped at the brutality of his questions and his lack of pity. 'Your profession, no doubt, makes you hard and without compassion,' she said at last. 'Whatever the outcome with Trevor, I'll adjust my plans accordingly when the time comes.'

'Well spoken.' His tone now was slightly jeering. 'I wish I could have taken such a sane view of life as a whole. Unfortunately, I've never been able to see more than a piece of it at a time.'

She reddened. 'I wasn't meaning to imply that I could look into the future and I am, of course, extremely grateful to you for accepting Trevor as a patient, whether there is a cure or not.'

She might just as well not have spoken, for he appeared to be reflecting on other matters. His cigar had gone out and he relit it. 'You'll have me confiding to you the story of my life soon if I don't watch out.'

'No, indeed, Mr. Mallory. I'm not expecting any revelations,' she said hastily, too hastily.

'You mean you're not interested in my long list of girls I once found attractive? Be careful, Felicity, I might exact a penance from you and condemn you to just such a recital.'

'As you please,' she answered politely. Let him spill the tales of his conquests, let him brag about his love-life strewn with broken hearts. She, at least, was immune and independent.

'You disapprove of my carefree attitude towards women, don't you?' he mocked.

'Should I disapprove? What makes you think so?'

'You have a certain rather prudish look in your eye and a very cool way of speaking sometimes. I find it quite disconcerting.'

'You find it nothing of the kind,' she snapped. 'You're trying to bait me into begging you to tell all.'

He laughed and lay back on the sand, pillowing his head behind his hands. 'I won't bore you. I'm not sure I can remember the faces, much less the names that matched. There was only one girl—and she—oh, never mind.'

He had rolled over and his face was averted from her. She did not speak, but her mind was a quick flurry of questions? Was this girl the real reason that he, too, had exiled himself on an island in the Adriatic? Or was it as Noel Bennett had told her, that Burne Mallory had been glad to escape the threat of scandal, a scandal that could wreck his profession?

After a long pause, he raised himself on one elbow and looked searchingly at her. 'What makes you so confoundedly calm and self-possessed? Don't you even want to know about her? The one girl I don't want to forget?'

'Not if it hurts you to talk about her.'

He moved lithely to his feet and lifted her by her elbows.

'Some other time.' He pulled her close towards him, kissed her abruptly and hard, then released her. 'I hope you're not taking that seriously?'

'Of course not. Should I?'

'There you go again with that holier-than-thou attitude!' he exclaimed. 'Come on. Let's go.'

He helped her up towards a rocky path that skirted the coast and it was only after some little time that she realised her hand was held firmly in Burne's grasp, but when the path narrowed, he released her and led the way.

After a short distance they came to another inlet, a narrow one with only a rock-strewn beach and a wooden staging that ran out into the deeper water. Several boats bobbed alongside the tiny pier and among them she could not fail to notice Burne's boat, *La Perla*.

'How did it get here?' she asked.

'Thought-transference,' he answered glibly. 'Waving magic wands is quite out of date now.'

'You instructed someone to untie from the place where we landed and bring it round here.'

He clapped his hands mockingly. 'Clever logical girl! We must use you to solve all our island mysteries.'

She began to walk towards the wooden pier, but he grabbed her arm. 'You're in too much of a hurry to get home,' he said sternly. 'First, we'll have some coffee. There's a café close by.'

They sat outside on a terrace where there were few other customers.

'I didn't realise that this little island had so many interesting places, coves and beaches and so on,' she said conversationally.

'It has more than that. Legends and stories to make your hair curl. Pirate-haunted for centuries, and even nowadays a bit of skulduggery goes on, so they say.' He broke off to wave to an acquaintance at a nearby table. 'Ah, Stefano!' A man's voice answered, but since the owner was behind Felicity, she could not turn to see Burne's friend.

When they were on the way back to Isola Rossa, Burne said, 'You've not asked me once today if I thought a cure was possible in your brother's case.'

She gazed up at him as he stood between the engine housing and the stern of the boat. 'If there's anything worth saying, I know that you'd tell me as soon as you could.'

He gave her a piercing look, but did not reply.

In the almost windless atmosphere, Isola Rossa seemed to sit on the water like a swan. 'It's not a painted ship but a painted island on a painted ocean,' she murmured.

'Don't you wonder what's behind the canvas, then?' he queried.

She laughed and shook her head. 'Could I see the rest of

44

your boat? I've never been on a cabin-cruiser before.'

'Why, of course! You funny girl! It's a lapse on my part. I should have taken you on a tour of inspection, but you'll have to go by yourself now. I have to steer for the harbour unless we want to hit the rocks.'

She went down the short companionway to the well-fitted cabin with deep upholstered seats that converted into sleeping bunks. A table bolted to the floor could be up-ended when not in use. There was a tiny galley with a cooking stove and sink, and every available inch of space had been utilised with cupboards.

'You could live here very comfortably,' she said to Burne when she reappeared. '*La Perla* has all mod. cons.'

'It's a thought that has crossed my mind—when I get tired of the gay life and the bright lights of Isola Rossa.'

He was nosing the boat into the harbour, expertly and surely, calling greetings to various fishermen in boats or on shore.

'Thank you for such a nice day,' she said, almost shyly, as they walked towards the place where his car was parked under an awning which appeared to be made of thick reeds woven into a screen.

He gave her a straight look in which amusement and a frowning impatience were mingled. 'Maybe we'll try it again some time, though you needn't construe that as a promise.'

'No, I won't,' she answered gently, as he slammed the car door his side and drove off.

When he reached the main gates of the clinic, he stopped. 'Mind if I drop you here? I've an appointment.'

'But of course.' She jumped out of the car hastily. 'Why didn't you say so? I could have walked up from the har-bour.'

He was already reversing the car and as he headed down the road again, he raised his hand to her and called, '*Ciao!*' She had learned that this strange word, sounding like '*Chow!*', was used indiscriminately for 'Hallo' or 'Goodbye' whenever Italians met or parted.

45

Burne's informal use of the word warmed her as she walked slowly along the main drive to the villa where she lived. What an extraordinary half-day it had been! Perhaps there would never be another quite like it, with Burne Mallory in so many different moods, mocking and gentle, demanding and impatient. There had been a strange, dreamlike quality about the afternoon which she would not easily forget.

At the entrance to the villa, Noel Bennett was just coming out.

'Had a good day?' he queried.

'Very pleasant,' she answered.

'Oh, Mallory can be quite charming when he chooses, but don't be misled. Remember what I told you,' he warned her.

Laughing, Felicity promised she would remember. It would be the worst possible consequence if she ever forgot that Burne Mallory made his own laws where women were concerned, and that a few hours spent in his company were merely his way of passing the time.

CHAPTER THREE

ISOBEL had been on duty all day, but she joined Felicity and Trevor for dinner. Luella and Maria were absent and Trevor was moody and silent. Isobel, on the other hand, was pleasantly gay and wanted to know all about Felicity's day out.

'Hendrik told me he had given you some time off. Did you enjoy yourself?'

Felicity nodded. 'Very much indeed.' She hoped that Isobel would not ask too many details, for Trevor was already annoyed because she had been on a trip in Mr. Mallory's boat.

'Did you go to one of the other islands?' pursued Isobel with relentless interest.

'Yes, to Rondine.'

'While I was stuck here opening and shutting my eyes for some silly notion!' exclaimed Trevor angrily.

Isobel smiled at him. 'Oh, it's more than likely that Mr. Mallory will take you for trips in his boat when he's satisfied with your progress. Although it must be said that Burne isn't all that generous with his excursions. He likes to pick and choose.'

'I think he only chose to take me today,' put in Felicity, 'because he was there when Dr. Johansen gave me the free time.'

'Then it was right for Burne to show you a little graciousness and give you a pleasant day. I've been out with him a few times and I know how genial he can be when he's in the right mood.' Isobel helped herself to a few cherries from the dish in the centre of the table. 'Of course, one must allow for his temperament.'

Felicity was only too glad when the meal was over and she and Trevor could escape from Isobel's amiable chatter.

'When can you arrange for me to go out in his boat?' were Trevor's first words when he and Felicity were alone on the latter's balcony.

'You know I can't *arrange* anything of the sort,' she answered. 'Mr. Mallory isn't an ogre. You can ask him yourself some time. He knows how keen you are on boats generally. He might even regard taking you on a trip as part of your treatment—if only to keep you in a good mood,' she ended, with a reassuring smile.

'Behind my back you went,' he fretted. 'It was a low-down trick.'

'It wasn't, Trevor,' she told him gently. 'I had no idea he was going to use his boat today. I thought he would just take me for a drive somewhere on this island, only because he had a free hour or so to while away.'

'Then let's go down to that harbour café now,' he suggested. 'I'm tired of being cooped up in this place all day and evening as well.'

Felicity agreed. She understood how boring it was for her young brother to be shut away from whatever life was going on outside.

She had discovered that a path through the clinic grounds led through a gate on to the road, thereby cutting off a considerable distance of the rougher part.

'How did you find this short cut?' Trevor asked as they emerged within sight of the twinkling lights of the harbour.

'Noel Bennett showed me,' she answered casually.

'Oh, I see. You've started on him, have you?' her brother teased. 'Going for twilight walks and all that. You won't have any luck there. He's nuts about Isobel.'

Felicity laughed. 'Can't one of the doctors even show me a path without your soaring imagination linking us together?'

At the café, which Felicity now saw was called *L'Aragosta*, its sign, a large red painted lobster, was translation enough, there were few people tonight either in the café itself or the outdoor part by the harbour wall. She would have been content to sit quietly in the darkened garden, but

48

Trevor wanted rather more noise and excitement.

Felicity ordered a flask of wine and she and Trevor had been sitting at a corner table for a short time when a dark-haired girl entered, accompanied by three young men. Trevor waved to the girl and called, 'Zia!' She came towards his table with a provocative swagger.

'Felicity, this is Zia.' Trevor introduced her. 'My sister.'

Zia, wearing a short black skirt and white silk blouse cut low off the shoulders, murmured, 'Sister. *Bene*.'

'Zia doesn't understand much English,' Trevor explained hurriedly.

Felicity smiled at the girl. 'Then that makes two of us. I don't understand much Italian.'

Zia sat down at the table in response to Trevor's invitation, but conversation between the three became spasmodic. They resorted to pantomimic gestures, but Felicity had the impression that language difficulties alone did not account entirely for the uneasiness which affected her. Zia was a very pretty girl with a round, full face, luscious lips and luminous dark eyes, but to Felicity she spelled danger and trouble.

Eventually, Trevor said, 'D'you mind if I dance with Zia?'

Felicity had no wish to be left alone, although the café seemed respectable enough, but something of her hesitation must have shown in her face, for Zia immediately grasped the situation. She spoke rapidly to Trevor, who understood no more than a word or two, then she darted off towards the men with whom she had first come into the café.

Trevor stared, then turned angrily towards his sister. 'There, now see what you've done. She's offended.'

But Zia was already returning with Tomaso, the taxi-driver, whom Felicity had already met once. Felicity hardly knew whether Zia's well-meaning action had improved matters or not, but at least Tomaso knew a fair amount of English.

While Trevor and Zia were dancing, Tomaso ordered more wine, Felicity produced her Italian phrase-book, and with a few hand-waving gestures, they managed to give each other lessons in pronunciation.

When Trevor and Zia rejoined them, there was much laughter at his attempts at Italian and Zia's exaggerated mouthing and poutings. The evening sped by on wings and when Felicity glanced at her watch she saw that it was now long past midnight.

'Come on, Trevor,' she urged. 'We shall be locked out.'

Zia trilled with laughter and said something that Tomaso translated as a reference to the fact that the clinic was no longer a monastery.

Reluctantly and a little unsteadily, Trevor rose. Felicity bit her lip in annoyance. She should have watched that he did not drink so much of the strong local wine.

'I can get my car,' Tomaso offered. 'It is late and the road is dark.'

'Oh, thank you, Tomaso, that's very kind of you.'

'Wait here,' he said, and went out of the café.

Zia gave Trevor a ravishing smile and called, '*Arrivederci,*' before she went across the room to rejoin her previous companions.

Trevor half rose from his chair into which he had subsided, but Felicity tugged at his coat. 'Don't interrupt her when she's with her own friends.'

A moment or two later Tomaso poked his head in the door and beckoned. Felicity steered Trevor safely past Zia's table, but not without one of those provocative glances from the girl, accompanied by a couple of remarks in Italian which made her companions laugh, but which Felicity did not comprehend.

It was good to be outside in the open air, after the heat and stuffiness of the café. She bundled Trevor into the car and stepped in after him. Tomaso was unusually silent on the short drive to the clinic, but perhaps, she thought, this was preferable to his talkativeness and erratic driving on the previous occasion.

'Stop at the main gates,' she instructed him. 'We can walk up the drive.' Tomaso's car with its snorting and banging would create too much disturbance and probably arouse all the patients and staff within earshot.

Once her eyes grew accustomed to the darkness, Felicity was able to guide her brother up to the villa, but she had not bargained for a meeting with Burne Mallory in the vestibule.

'You're late prowlers, aren't you?' he greeted them.

'We went to the harbour café, the one called *L'Aragosta*, and we stayed rather a long time,' she explained.

'Not long enough for me,' declared Trevor. '*Buona sera!*' he called jauntily to Burne, and went towards the stairs.

'Listen, Felicity,' said Burne in a low, urgent voice. 'I don't want to play the heavy father over an occasional evening's enjoyment, but you must co-operate with me if I'm even to try to help you brother. He needs rest before I start the treatment I have in mind.'

'Well, he's only danced a little in the café. Most of the time we sat at a table and Tomaso drove us up here.'

'He wears dark glasses during the day—or I hope he does—but at night he probably takes them off, so his eyes have to keep adjusting to all kinds of artificial light.'

'Surely you don't mean that he isn't to go out at night?' she queried.

'That's exactly what I do mean,' he snapped.

'But it's unreasonable to expect a boy of his age to be cooped up all day and then be forbidden to have a little relaxation in the evening.' She was protesting about his apparent unfairness, but she knew that she was on anything but firm ground, as Burne's next words proved.

'The choice is entirely yours, Felicity. Either you want at least the chance of a cure for your brother or your irresponsibility will defeat the object of coming here to the clinic.'

She was silent for a moment or two. 'Of course, I realise that for the best results, Trevor must put himself entirely into your hands and obey your wishes, but it's going to be hard for me to restrain him on every occasion and keep him

51

shut up at nights.'

Burne smiled. 'Try your powers of persuasion.'

Felicity glanced up to catch the tail-end of that sardonic smile. 'Wouldn't a definite order come better from you? He'll accuse me of being his gaoler.'

'No. I want you to do your best. It'll be good practice for you. At most times in your life you'll be persuading some man or other to do what you want him to do, so why not exert yourself on Trevor's behalf now? Besides, you'll be doing me a service. Doesn't that count?'

She gave him a wry smile. 'I know when I'm beaten,' she murmured. 'All right, I'll do as you say.'

She left him without more than a casual, *'Buona sera,'* to which he answered with emphasis, *'Buona notte.'* She recognised that he was correcting her in the proper use of the phrases, for *'Buona notte'* meant a definite 'Good night' when people were going to bed.

What sort of a good night's sleep did Burne Mallory think she could enjoy when he had landed her with such a problem? Yet in her heart she knew he was right. Trevor would have to be firmly handled and she must not fail to impress on him the importance of resigning himself to Mr. Mallory's demands.

She and Trevor usually ate their breakfast on Trevor's balcony, an arrangement that had the advantage of waking him up at a reasonable time before Felicity had to dress and start work for Dr. Johansen. In London, Felicity had often left him in bed when she went out in the mornings, but here the cool, sunny mornings were such a delight that, as she often told him, it was a pity to miss them.

'Have you any treatment planned for today?' she asked him the next morning after their late night out.

'No,' he answered with a yawn. 'Tomorrow I have to be stuck indoors, so I'm going out today.'

'Where?'

She was alerted by something in his face. He sounded as though he had a definite plan in view.

'Only down to the harbour. Perhaps I'll swim in the cove

on the other side.'

'You'll be back to lunch?' she queried.

'Probably not. I'll get something at the café or maybe I'll go to Mariano's.'

'All right. Come back in good time for dinner, though, in case Mr. Mallory wants to discuss something with you about tomorrow's treatment.'

'O.K., sister.' He grinned boyishly at her. 'Fusspot!'

She was uncertain whether to tell him about Mr. Mallory's ban on being out after dark, but decided not to say anything yet. Tonight she would induce him to stay at the clinic and no doubt his ambition to watch the harbour life would be satisfied if he spent most of the day down there. The prospect of a good dinner might also beckon him, for Trevor had acquired a fondness for Italian cooking and enjoyed the spicy *pizzas, ravioli* dishes and fritters that Sofia, the housekeeper at the villa, cooked so well.

Today was exceptionally busy in Dr. Johansen's office and she worked hard and willingly in return for the free time she had been given yesterday.

Trevor did not appear for lunch, but she had not expected him. She stayed until after seven in the evening to finish some long reports, then returned to the villa, expecting Trevor to be there. He was not in his room, but possibly he was roaming about in the grounds of the clinic.

When he did not come in for dinner, Felicity asked Luella if she had seen him.

The young nurse replied that she had not, but would enquire at Mr. Mallory's clinic.

'No,' said Felicity hastily. 'He wasn't to attend at Mr. Mallory's today. Oh, well, I suppose he'll come in soon.'

By the time dinner was over and darkness had fallen, there was still no sign of the boy, and Felicity was really worried. She should have impressed on him that he was to be home in the daylight.

Isobel offered to look in the main building in case he had gone there to chat with other patients, but Felicity guessed that was a slender hope.

'He wouldn't be wandering about the grounds now in the dark,' she said to Isobel. 'I'll have to go down to the harbour and look for him.'

'I'll come with you, if you like,' Isobel offered.

Felicity was quite prepared to walk down the rough, stony road, but as soon as Noel heard of Trevor's absence, he offered to drive both girls and lost no time in getting out the car.

'Call first at Mariano's,' advised Isobel, when they approached the harbour. 'He's the gossip exchange around here. Always knows what's going on.'

Mariano admitted that he had seen Trevor just before noon but not since. 'He said he might go fishing with Tomaso.'

'Well, he's not out fishing now, that's obvious,' declared Noel.

At the harbour café, *L'Aragosta*, there was no sign of the boy, and Felicity's hopes fell, for she had confidently expected to find him at what was apparently Trevor's favourite haunt.

'Let's try Gino's,' suggested Noel, 'but I'll have to leave the car here.'

He guided Felicity and Isobel up a narrow alley, unlit except for an occasional shaft of light from an open doorway. A sharp turn led up a steep flight of steps and about halfway up two small lanterns in the shape of pomegranates glowed outside a doorway.

Noel pushed open the door and the girls followed him down some steps, along a passage and through another door.

The noise and the smoke-filled atmosphere made Felicity recoil. 'Yes, there's always rather a racket going on,' whispered Isobel.

Through the smoke Felicity saw a number of tables with men drinking or chatting. Only a few girls were there and most of them were dancing with partners on the small cleared space in the middle of the room.

A waiter sidled up to Noel, held up his fingers to indicate

a table for three and conducted Noel and the two girls to one in a corner.

'We must have something to drink,' explained Noel, to Felicity, 'to give us the chance to look around.'

'Is this the place you spoke of?' she asked Isobel. 'You said it had a rather dubious character.'

Isobel nodded. 'Nothing very outrageous, you understand. No one gets up and starts knifing someone else—at least, not often!' She laughed. 'But it's known on the island as a kind of meeting place for those who want to get mixed up with shady business. Apart from that, it's no worse than many an English pub. Some of those can be pretty grim with smoke and noise.'

Felicity nodded. She was raising her glass to her lips when she suddenly stiffened. 'I heard Trevor's laugh,' she said. 'Somewhere near by.'

'I'll go and look,' Noel offered. The two girls watched him make a leisurely tour of the room as though he were idly looking for a friend. He came back a few moments later. 'No sign of him.'

'Something's happened to him,' murmured Felicity in despair. 'Some accident. Perhaps he and Tomaso haven't returned from fishing. They could be out there somewhere in the sea.'

When they had finished the wine, Felicity was eager to leave. 'We must tell the police. They might know about an accident.'

Isobel said kindly, 'The police force here is not very large. Two men. One of them is the equivalent of a sergeant, I suppose. His mate has only one eye and is often said to be blind in the other. But we'll try.'

As they rose to go, Felicity stopped. 'There! I'm sure that was Trevor's laugh.'

She moved quickly away from the table, went round a corner where a jutting wall made a small alcove.

'Trevor!' she called sharply.

His back was towards her and he turned slowly and blinked at her. His companion, Zia, giggled with mock

55

dismay.

'Seester!' she spluttered, then made motions as though to shoo away Trevor.

'Good lord!' exclaimed Trevor. 'What are you doing here?'

'I might ask you that,' returned Felicity evenly, determined not to lose her temper. 'You could at least have telephoned that you were not coming back to dinner.'

'Oh, for heaven's sake!' Trevor burst out impatiently. 'I don't see why I have to be followed around all the time. If you want to know, I went out fishing with Tomaso and it was late when we came back, so Zia kindly invited me to her place for a meal, then we came on here. Anything disgraceful in that?'

'No, except that you're not supposed to be out at night.'

'Who says so?'

'Mr. Mallory. You're his patient and he expects you to co-operate.' Felicity stopped talking, aware that so far she had not impressed on Trevor Mr. Mallory's latest instructions. 'You'd better come along with us now.'

By this time Noel and Isobel had joined Felicity and somehow this seemed to anger Trevor.

'I'll be damned if I'll meekly crawl home when you send out a search party for me.' He sat down in his chair, but in the semi-darkness missed his balance and the chair tilted, sending him sprawling against the wall.

Noel hauled the boy to his feet. 'Don't be a damned fool, Trevor. Come now and don't make a fuss. You'll have plenty of time for these night spots when your eyes have been cured.'

Felicity noticed that Zia had silently disappeared. No doubt the girl was skilful at avoiding trouble when it arose.

Noel paid the waiter for Trevor's wine and helped him out into the dark alley.

'You shamed me before the whole lot of them!' Trevor exclaimed, directing his remark to Felicity who was a step or two behind. 'Collecting me as though I were a small child at a party!'

56

'Then why didn't you let someone know where you were?' retorted Felicity, although she felt she had handled the situation badly. She had behaved tactlessly, even if her reasons were sound and sincere. She must remember in future that her 'kid brother' was developing a man's pride, even though he sometimes behaved like a stupid schoolboy.

She noticed now how unsteady Trevor was on his feet, but she had no means of knowing whether that was due to his lack of good sight or to the amount of wine he had been drinking.

In the car Noel made casual conversation with Trevor next to him, but Felicity and Isobel were silent in the back seats. When Felicity began a sentence, Isobel shook a warning finger at her.

Noel stopped outside the villa and while Felicity was thanking him and Isobel for their help, Dr. Johansen strolled across from the main building.

'Ah, you are all back together,' he said contentedly. 'That is satisfactory.'

Felicity managed to murmur that they had met Trevor in the little town, but behind Dr. Johansen she saw Burne Mallory approaching.

Noel drove the car to put it away in the garage, Isobel disappeared into the villa, Trevor was leaning against the doorway.

'Had a good day, Trevor?' Burne enquired, as though it were the one thing he wanted to know.

'Marvellous,' answered Trevor, innocently rising to the bait. 'At least, it was until Felicity came and winkled me out of——'

'Trevor went out fishing,' put in Felicity, trying to forestall her brother's untimely disclosures.

'In the dark?' queried Burne.

'Tomaso showed me how to find the shoals,' Trevor continued, ignoring Burne's question. 'I'm going to hire a boat for myself. Tomaso has friends, he says, who'll let me have one.'

'You'll do no such thing,' said Burne in a voice that

rasped. 'D'you really think I'm going to waste my time on trying to find a cure for your particular eye trouble and let you go roaming all over the Adriatic any time of day or night?' He swerved towards Felicity. 'As for you, I asked you only last night to try to co-operate, and you haven't even tried.'

'I—let me explain,' began Felicity.

'I don't want explanations. I want obedience and strict supervision if I'm going to continue with any kind of treatment. May I remind you both that I have other patients to attend to? People who really care about their sight?'

He marched across the wide, paved drive, leaving Felicity shaken and apprehensive.

Dr. Johansen took her arm. 'Don't be too upset, Miss Hilton. Where his profession is concerned, Mr. Mallory is very serious-minded.' He smiled. 'Sometimes his manner is rather abrupt, and you must forgive him.'

'I'm the one to blame,' Felicity admitted quietly. 'I didn't warn Trevor when I ought to have done. Thank you, Dr. Johansen. Good night.'

Trevor had already strolled into the villa and Felicity accompanied him upstairs to his room.

'Who does he think he is, Mr. High-and-Mighty?' grumbled Trevor as he sank into a chair. 'He's only able to chuck his weight about like that because there's no other specialist near. In London or anywhere else, his patients would soon clear off if he spoke to them like that.'

'It was partly my fault,' Felicity said. 'He asked me to try to keep an eye on you at night-time, because of the changing light. I didn't tell you soon enough, but of course I didn't know you were going to be out this evening as well as in the daytime.'

Trevor appeared not to be listening. 'Come to think of it,' he muttered, continuing his own train of thought, 'I wonder what he's doing here in this glamorous spot. I'll bet there's something shady in his past or he wouldn't be here.'

Felicity smiled. 'You can hardly expect him to confess his reasons to us.' It occurred to her, however, that while

58

Burne had asked her point-blank who or what she was running away from, he had not indicated his own reasons. All he had hinted was that there had been a girl, the one girl that he didn't want to forget.

'Come on, Trevor,' she urged. 'Go to bed and get a decent night's sleep. Treatment day tomorrow.'

'Exactly. So I can hardly be blamed if I went out and enjoyed myself today. I'm going to have that boat, though, whatever Mallory says.'

'Not until he gives you permission,' she snapped. 'Be patient, Trevor. For heaven's sake, give yourself a chance!'

He yawned. 'All right. But there's nothing and nobody to stop me going out in Tomaso's boat or anyone else's. I might even take Lord High-and-Mighty's little fancy job and go out for a ride.'

'Nonsense!' Felicity chuckled, but she was too cautious to mention that Trevor wouldn't dare to take the motor-cruiser. In his present circumstances, her brother would regard that as a challenge to foolishness.

When she was summoned to Mr. Mallory's clinic the following morning, she hurried there, anxious to know what attitude Burne would take after last night's reprimands.

Prepared to find him coolly abrupt, she was surprised when he welcomed her with one of his most charming smiles.

'Now, you two,' he addressed them both when Trevor arrived in charge of a nurse, 'I want to talk very straightly. I take it, Trevor, that you really want to be cured, if a cure can be found?'

'Naturally,' the boy answered.

'You want to be able to live a life of your own, go in for sports, make some sort of career?'

'Yes.'

'Then, in that case, put yourself entirely in my hands.' Burne's voice was very gentle. 'In less than a year, or at the most, two years, you'll be completely blind, even if you do nothing to accelerate the process. Give me at least a month and I may be able to do something for you.'

'A cure?' interposed Felicity, unable to restrain her eager query.

'No promises.' Burne gave her a level look, then turned back to Trevor. 'One month, at least, I demand. Even under strict supervision, life need not be hopelessly dull for you, but no night outings at all, no giggles with Italian girls in smoky cafés, and not too much of the good red wine so abundant here.'

Trevor grimaced. 'The simple life with a vengeance! I'm told this place was once a monastery.'

'After that it was a summer palace of a nobleman, so I'd say that monastic austerity gave place to rather more gracious living,' replied Burne caustically. 'Well, is it a deal? Or don't you care if you go blind?'

Felicity saw Burne's warning glance and bit back her impulse to say that of course Trevor cared very much.

Trevor sighed, then smiled. 'I'll do as you say. I promise.'

'Thanks,' muttered Burne, with one eyebrow uplifted.

'Also, I apologise for last night,' Trevor added, with a disarming grin, as colour reddened his face. 'I just let Tomaso jolly me along with him to the café. I had the world's outsize in headaches this morning.'

'That's not surprising,' was Burne's grim comment. 'Now you can have a certain amount of freedom in the daytime, except for those times when I want to examine your eyes. But understand that the harbour and its cafés are out of bounds. Boats, too, for that matter.'

Trevor's face indicated that he was prepared to resign himself to a period with no fun at all. 'Roll on the next two months,' he said gaily, and Felicity was relieved that at last her brother was willing to co-operate.

When she had left Trevor in the care of a nurse, Burne accompanied her to the door of his clinic.

'You probably won't answer me,' she began, 'but have you any kind of operation in mind?'

He looked at her with a fixed expression, as though he were considering his answer. 'An operation may be neces-

60

sary, but even that doesn't guarantee a cure.'

'I'm aware of that. I'm not trying to make you commit yourself,' she assured him.

'Committing myself is something I never do—either professionally or personally.' His eyes glinted with amusement. 'Don't worry, Felicity. Unless your brother makes a complete fool of himself, I expect to be able to do something to help his sight improve.'

She returned to Dr. Johansen's office lighter in heart than she had felt for some time. Trevor's promise to behave sensibly meant a load off her mind.

As she worked she must have been humming a tune, for when Noel Bennett came into the room he asked, 'Why so happy? Or are you always our little ray of sunshine?'

'I am this morning, Noel,' she answered. 'At last I believe there's some real hope of a cure for my brother's possible blindness.'

'Oh? Did Burne Mallory tell you that?'

'Yes, of course.'

'Don't put your entire faith in the man. He's brilliant, I know, and has made some spectacular cures, but there have been one or two cases where he's failed.'

'Oh, Noel, don't cut the ground from under my feet!' she begged, although she did not think he was being very serious. Because of his personal attitude about Isobel, he often took this line of belittling Burne Mallory.

'It's just that I don't want you to be disappointed in the end. Well, let's talk about something else. How about coming out with me this evening? There isn't much to do in the place, I know, but we could dance perhaps at the *Aragosta*.'

Felicity looked up at this very attractive young doctor with his square-cut chin, thick, curly hair and brown eyes.

An evening out in his company would have been most welcome, but tonight of all nights, she considered it unwise and tactless to spend her free time with anyone but Trevor.

'Some other time?' she queried, smiling at Noel. 'I must stay home with Trevor tonight. You know how much trouble we both got into with Mr. Mallory over last night, so I'd better not blot my copy-book again.'

'Blot your——' he began, in clear astonishment.

'Oh, I didn't mean that. Not coming out with you. But going out with anyone would seem rather unkind to my brother tonight.'

'I don't think you need shut yourself up in a nunnery on that account.' Burne's voice made both Felicity and Noel turn round sharply. Neither had heard him come in the room. 'I'm going out in my boat this evening. Want to come?'

Felicity's colour rose in her cheeks as she glanced at Noel, who shrugged his broad shoulders and went quickly out of the room.

'I asked you a question,' Burne persisted.

'I know. I'm thinking of the answer.'

'You can say "yes" or "no", can't you? Where did Noel want to take you?'

'He asked me to go dancing at the *Aragosta*,' she said coolly. 'I didn't say "yes" or "no". I told him "some other time".'

'Well, you now have my permission to go out if you want to. Trevor won't come to any harm tonight.'

'Where is he?'

'He'll be in my clinic, with a nurse in constant attendance and all visitors barred. So you're quite free tonight.'

'Thank you,' she said, failing to keep the irony out of her voice.

Burne moved away from the filing cabinet where he had been standing. 'Let me know if you've a mind to go dancing or boating.'

He was almost at the door when she said defiantly, 'I could always wash my hair or give myself a manicure.'

He turned with a smile that surprised her by its warmth. 'Typical redhead!' he gibed. 'Always up in arms against something. Although really you're not truly typical. Your eyes have no right to be blue. They should be green or brown or some other colour.'

'As an eye specialist you should know that we can't easily

62

change the colour of our eyes to suit a passing whim of an acquaintance.'

He was now in the middle of the office and he began to laugh, not his usual sardonic chuckle, but a deep-throated sound as though he were enjoying a huge joke. After a moment or two, she joined in the laughter.

'I'll be ready about six,' he said incisively as he went out of the door.

Felicity's laughter stopped suddenly in mid-breath. She stared at the half-finished report in her typewriter. How on earth could she accept Burne's invitation when she had already refused Noel's? She could easily tell Noel that she would be glad to go dancing with him, so what was it that prevented her from doing so? Why did she sit back and let events take charge of her instead of making her own decisions?

She picked up the telephone and asked for Dr. Bennett.

'He's not here,' a voice answered. 'He's gone out. I think he said he was going to the mainland to pick up some equipment.'

'Any idea when he will be back?' queried Felicity.

'No. Not until late this evening, probably. Can I take a message?'

'No, it's all right.' Felicity replaced the phone.

Really, it was not all right, for she experienced a spark of satisfaction that Noel was absent, thus cancelling one element of choice. Now she was left with accepting or declining Burne's invitation, request, demand or whatever name might be given to his casual words, 'I'll be ready at six.'

It was not yet midday, so she had until five o'clock to decide.

63

CHAPTER FOUR

FROM the deck of *La Perla* the dark outline of Isola Rossa against the evening sky could be distinguished mainly because nearer the water line the long hump of land was stabbed with lights in a cluster by the harbour, dying away to isolated ones or twos stretching along the roads away from the town.

On board Burne's boat, Felicity called herself several kinds of hypocrite, for at six o'clock she had needed no further persuasion. She had been ready and now here she was, accompanied by Burne, but shadowed also by a nagging thought that she allowed herself to be picked up too easily by Burne. With a quiet smile to herself, she decided that he would just as easily drop her when the time came or when a fresh face appeared over his horizon.

'What are you smiling at?' Burne interrupted her thoughts.

'Was I? I didn't know. Perhaps because I appreciate the peacefulness of being out in a boat at night-time.'

'Another of those evasive answers of yours,' he commented. 'That chap was right when he said that words were given us so that we could hide our thoughts.'

'It could be that I was meditating on your excellence as a cook.'

He had told her that he would knock up a snack meal on board. 'Waiting for dinner or having a meal in a café is often a waste of time when you could be eating it on the water and watching a spectacular sunset at the same time.'

Tonight he had cruised towards Isola Rondine and anchored offshore. Then in the tiny galley he had heated soup, served a dish of veal with mushrooms accompanied by fried artichokes, followed by fruit salad and cheese. They had eaten without ceremony from trays on their laps,

Burne racing up the companionway from the saloon each time to prevent the food from cooling too soon. They had shared a bottle of Soave, a dry white wine, which Burne said was really a 'fish wine' as Felicity could see from the small cardboard fish dangling round the neck of the bottle.

While they were eating, Felicity found her attention divided between Burne's delicious food and the spectacular sunset he had prophesied.

From minute to minute the colours changed, orange to pink, towering masses of flame clouds turning to mauve, then dying to wild tawny streaks reflected brilliantly in the sea.

'I brought you to this spot,' Burne explained, 'so that you'd have an uninterrupted view.'

Now the last vestiges of daylight had disappeared, leaving a warm, velvety sky pricked with stars.

From somewhere on Isola Rondine came the sound of a guitar, followed by a man's voice singing what sounded like a passionate love song. The liquid, sensuous notes drifted across the water, needing no understanding of the language to comprehend the throbbing ardour of the phrases.

But Felicity, aware of the magic, the enchantment of moments like these, steeled herself against the sweet rapture that had come perilously close. When she glanced across at Burne, she saw in the ray of the masthead light that he was watching her, a cigar between his lips, his eyes hidden by the angle at which the light shone down.

She smiled at the thought that doubtless Burne had taken plenty of other girls out in his boat on warm, still nights, a feature of the softening-up process before conquest.

It occurred to her, however, that Burne was one of those people who had the gift of companionable silence. She did not feel it was necessary to make conversation for the sake of it.

A voice called quietly, '*Signore!*' answered by Burne's equally quiet '*Si!*' and almost immediately a small boat glided up alongside *La Perla*. A squarish box changed hands, Burne muttered a phrase or two and the boatman moved away as noiselessly as he had come. Burne took the box and put it below in the cabin.

A few moments later he asked, 'Are you cold? We'd better be moving, I think.'

Without waiting for her reply, he hauled up the anchor, allowed the boat to drift away from the island, then started the engine.

Felicity turned her face away from him. So it was not just a matter of idling the evening away and inviting her to share it. There had been a definite purpose in view, for obviously the boatman had brought his parcel by appointment. Equally obviously, Burne was anxious to get away now that the mission was accomplished. She almost laughed aloud. Her thoughts were clothing themselves in the language of a spy story!

'Most girls would have been agog to know what was happening,' he said, when after some minutes *La Perla* rounded the tip of the island and headed for the strip of sea between Rondine and Lupa.

'I won't say I'm not interested,' returned Felicity. 'That parcel could contain almost anything, innocent or suspicious. Let us say, a few tins of food or some bottles of wine. Or you might be engaged in a shuttle service of library books on exchange.'

Burne laughed. 'Why at this time of night?'

'Because the librarian is also a fisherman and works in the daytime,' she retorted quickly. 'On the other hand, he or his accomplices, might be forgers and the case contains bundles of ten-thousand-lire notes. I don't know what else would be smuggled around these parts. Tobacco, possibly?'

'Your imagination is working overtime,' he told her. 'For a really lively smuggler, there are endless possibilities among islands like these. There's always gold, although the darned stuff is so heavy that you have to be careful it doesn't sink the boat.'

She joined in his laughter. 'I'm not really prying. It's your business.'

'So it is,' he agreed, 'but for two pins I'd make you a

66

partner in my smuggling racket. You understand, of course, that I don't own this kind of boat for nothing.'

'Naturally. You need something fast to evade such people as customs officers or rival smugglers.'

His laughter rang out as they now came within sight of Isola Rossa again.

'You don't really think I'm capable of skulduggery?' he queried.

'Certainly. I think you're quite capable of anything that suits your purpose at the time,' she answered lightly.

'H'm. Then it's no use asking you to be a witness for the defence if I'm hauled up before the courts.'

'You wouldn't want me to perjure myself, I'm sure.'

Somewhere in Felicity's thoughts an undercurrent of caution warned her not to carry this delicious fooling too far. She must still try to keep that delicate balance with Burne and not let friendliness develop into a provocative attitude.

At Isola Rossa he moored to a part of the quay where the water was only a foot or so below the wall. After tying up, he lithely scrambled ashore, then helped Felicity, grasping her by the arms, then around her waist before he set her down.

'The parcel!' she reminded him, as they crossed the quay. 'Have you forgotten it?'

He grinned. 'Someone will arrive at a chosen hour, step down on to my boat, pick up the hot money, stolen jewels, ticking bomb or whatever it is and then—melt into the darkness! Come on, let's drink to his success.'

He guided her towards Mariano's bar and ordered wine.

'Don't let Trevor know that I've been out again in your boat,' she said after a while. 'He's so keen himself to be invited. It makes him restive if he can't go.'

Burne smiled at her across the table. 'A bargain! I'll keep your secrets if you'll keep mine,' he teased.

'Thank you.'

There were only four or five men in the bar and Mariano was affable to all, but Felicity noticed that whenever she

67

glanced his way, his dark eyes swerved away, as though he did not wish to be caught staring, yet when she and Burne left the bar with a few words exchanged between him and Mariano, the Italian's gaze was bold and direct. His smile was friendly enough as he wished her, '*Buona sera*,' but she wondered if he were mentally sizing her up as just another of the Signor Mallory's girl-friends.

Burne had not brought his car tonight, for he and Felicity had walked through the grounds to the short cut that led to the harbour.

Now he asked, 'Are you tired? Can you manage to stagger up to your villa?'

She laughed. 'What will you do if I say I can't?' Then she blushed as she realised the implication of that inane remark. 'No, you needn't tell me,' she added quickly. 'I can walk quite well, since I've been sitting down most of the evening.'

'Why shouldn't I tell you?' he demanded. 'I could quite well leave you here to manage as best you could. Or I could try to ferret out Tomaso for his taxi, except that I happen to know he isn't available.'

'Gone smuggling, I expect,' she said, laughing. 'Goodness, you are ruthless, aren't you?'

By now they had walked to where a piece of stone wall skirted the edge of the hill road and Burne leaned against it. 'Look, Felicity,' he pointed across the sea. 'There goes the steamer on its way to Ancona.'

She could see the small cluster of moving lights far out to sea.

'What a world this must have been for hundreds of years with pirates coming ashore when you least expected it!' he murmured softly. 'On the other side of the Adriatic, what is now Dalmatia or Albania, it was just as bad. Worse, perhaps, because there are so many islands strung out all along those coasts, capable of giving shelter or hiding all kinds of ruffians.'

'Why did they go in for pirating?' she asked. 'They had territories of their own, didn't they?'

'Same reasons applied, I suppose, to the Danes, the Jutes, the Saxons and all the rest who raided ancient Britain. They saw some place where the grass was greener or their own bit of country became too hot for them, so they set out in their long-boats. It provided the excuse for a session of excitement and a relief from boredom.'

'They weren't always too gentle,' Felicity reminded him. 'They didn't mind whom they killed or whose house they burned.'

'Would you expect pirates to have such finer feelings? These three islands were probably convenient stopping places to rest before they attacked the mainland. That's why there are so many legends and tales around here. Isola Rondine, for instance. There's a small cave on the far side from here, where on certain nights of the year, so they say, you can hear the clang of swords, the cries and screams of the victims, then the sound of a boat drawing away.'

'I believe you're making it all up,' Felicity accused him.

'Indeed, I'm not!' he retorted with mock indignation. 'Ask Hendrik, if you don't believe me. He's soaked in all these legends. He can't forget his own Nordic ancestry. He can tell you sagas about the exploits of the Vikings and many of the tribes who followed them in other parts of Europe.'

'Isn't it a pity that so much history is concerned with plundering and violence? You never hear much about people living their quiet lives in peace.'

'Uneventful lives don't makes news. Only events do that, as any news reporter would tell you.' In the darkness she could see only the faintest silhouette of his features.

'Why did Dr. Johansen establish his clinic on this little island?' she asked, unsure whether Burne would tell her the truth even if he knew.

'That's a long story. He was on the deck of a steamer sailing down the Adriatic when he saw Isola Rossa and exclaimed, "*Eureka!* That's where I'll have my clinic."'

'Rubbish!' she retorted. 'He's not at all like that.'

'How right you are! Hendrik is nothing if not deliberate.

69

Everything he does is well planned, well thought out with provision for all possible snags. Well, the clinic is the outcome of ideas from the World Health Organisation, the Italian Government and several other interested parties. It began with chest cases and Hendrik had the bright idea that planting a hospital on a small island would considerably reduce the risk of infection and cross-infection from visitors. Also, it would enable comparisons to be made with the progress of patients in the high altitudes, such as north Italy, Switzerland and so on. Clean sea air might be just as beneficial, so Hendrik argued.'

'How long has he been here?' Felicity asked.

'Six or seven years, I think. He found this old palace that had once been a monastery, the owners were glad to be rid of it because of the upkeep and sold it to a medical organisation that comes partly under the Government. Hendrik was put in charge and he has absolute power. He can engage us and sack us as he pleases. He's virtually the hiring and firing boss.'

'He seems like a gentle tyrant to me,' observed Felicity.

'Hey! Are you falling for his tall Swedish build and fair-haired handsome looks?' Burne demanded.

'No, I don't think so. I'm not the kind of girl who assumes automatically that she must fall in love with her boss.'

'Take my advice and steer clear of the man,' he warned her. 'Your predecessor made that fatal mistake and the next thing she knew she was packed off to England.'

Felicity turned quickly to look at him, although she could see nothing of Burne's expression. 'The girl called Jill? I don't know her other name.'

'That's the one. Oh, she was quite pretty—in a chocolate-box way, but Hendrik is not the kind to be set on fire by an attractive face and a charming manner. He's far too dedicated to his work to allow for distractions of any kind.'

'Even dedicated doctors sometimes find time to marry,' she said mildly.

'Not this one. Not Hendrik Johansen.' Burne's tone was

70

decisive. After a pause, he said, 'Come on, let's go. You're probably getting cold.'

As they walked along the path through the grounds, Felicity was thoughtful about those last few remarks of Burne's. Noel had definitely told her that the girl Jill had developed an unfortunate infatuation for Burne Mallory, not Hendrik. Now Burne was declaring that Hendrik was the attraction. Was this Burne's way of disclaiming any kind of responsibility? She had heard that derogatory note in his voice when he had said that Jill was 'pretty—in a chocolate-box way'. No modern girl ever wants to be likened to such a style and she wondered what Burne's opinion of her own looks might be, although she did not have the courage to ask him.

For several days after this trip in Burne's boat, Felicity spent her available time with Trevor. At first he was allowed to walk out in the grounds and Felicity made a point of meeting him in the daytime whenever she could. Eventually, Burne decided that Trevor must remain indoors in the clinic, even though he need not necessarily lie in bed all day.

'I wish he could hurry up and find out what he's going to do,' complained Trevor one evening to Felicity.

'You can be sure that he's not going to keep you here longer than he needs to,' she reassured him. 'He's probably got a long waiting-list of patients eager to come.'

'Some of them must have pretty long journeys,' he remarked. 'It's not like going to London to Harley Street, is it?'

'No, but I expect people who need this treatment make the effort to come.'

Isobel seemed to be interested in the fact that Felicity had voluntarily tied up her free time with Trevor. Perhaps she felt happier with Felicity out of the way where Burne was concerned, although she need have no fears.

'I'm going over to the mainland tomorrow,' she announced one evening at dinner. 'Anything I can bring back for you?' she asked Felicity.

'Nothing I can think of at this moment,' Felicity answered, 'but perhaps I could let you know later?'

Isobel nodded. 'Of course, the shops over there aren't exactly on a level with London or Rome or Brighton, but they do stock a few more articles than one can buy here.'

The clinic had a well-stocked general store for the use of patients and staff. Felicity had found it decidedly useful since she and Trevor had travelled comparatively lightly and soon needed replacements of everyday cosmetics and the oddments one always needs when away from home.

There was no one else tonight in the dining-room at the villa and Isobel seemed in a talkative mood.

'How do you get on with Burne Mallory?' she asked.

'All right,' answered Felicity warily.

'All right as long as you're not on the wrong end of his terrible temper?'

'You mean when I had to go out and rescue Trevor that night. Well, perhaps Mr. Mallory'—Felicity stopped herself in time from saying 'Burne'—'had a right to be thoroughly annoyed with my brother and with me. We brought that on ourselves.'

'Burne doesn't always care whether his rage is justified or not,' commented Isobel. 'He's difficult to understand. I suppose that's one of the characteristics that makes him so attractive to girls.'

'Every girl believes that she's the privileged one that really will understand a difficult man,' replied Felicity calmly. She had no idea where this conversation was leading, but she surmised that the object was to warn her off Isobel's territory. 'D'you think that sometimes men pretend they're unpredictable just so that they can test out the girls?'

Across the table she met Isobel's eyes and both girls laughed.

'You sound quite an old hand!' murmured Isobel admiringly. 'Where did you learn your excellent philosophy?'

'Nowhere in particular.'

'But you were engaged, weren't you?'

Felicity frowned slightly. 'Not definitely engaged. We planned to be married in due course, but——'

'I suppose it was Trevor who was the difficulty?' asked Isobel sympathetically. 'It's really quite a problem for you, but at least if your brother recovers his proper sight, it's a problem that will disappear. I hope Burne makes a good cure.'

'So do I, with all my heart, but more for Trevor's sake than my own.'

'Burne took you out in his boat the other night, didn't he?' pursued Isobel casually.

'Yes. A moonlight trip, only it was a very dark night and there was no moon.'

Isobel laughed quietly. 'That's his usual ploy. First, the daylight outing, then dinner aboard—and he's so proud of his cooking!—followed by a cruise round the islands in the warm, velvety darkness. Oh, he's so keen to pretend that he's hard and cynical, but at heart he's a romantic.'

'Are you trying to warn me that he's a dangerous man?' Felicity asked Isobel, amusement dancing in her eyes. 'I've already been warned by Noel that I ought to look out that I don't burn my fingers.'

Isobel laughed, too, as she stood up and put her hand lightly on Felicity's shoulder. 'No, I don't think there's any need to warn you. You're much too sensible to be taken in by Burne's flattering attentions or his methods of repelling in order to attract more forcibly.'

'You seem to have developed quite a philosophy yourself, Isobel,' said Felicity.

'And besides, fortunately for you, you're not really Burne's type, I think,' continued Isobel.

'Beware, my girl,' Felicity warned the other mockingly, 'beware that I don't take that remark as a challenge and set out to entrap the man!'

Isobel's hand applied friendly pressure to Felicity's shoulder. 'That'll be worth watching, pet. If you're successful, let me know your methods, will you?' Her laughter was suddenly stifled and her hand dropped away from the other girl's shoulder.

Felicity, instantly aware of some sudden tension, turned her head to find Burne lounging in the doorway of the dining-room. How long had he been there? How much of this friendly, lighthearted conversation had he heard? Surely Isobel could not have known he was there until this moment.

'I came to ask what time you wanted to start tomorrow for the mainland.' He addressed Isobel, ignoring Felicity.

'Early, if possible. Seven o'clock? Half past?' Isobel answered with perfect calm.

'Right. We'll say seven, then we might get away by half past.' Burne bent one of his most alluring glances on Isobel's beautifully tanned face. 'If you're not ready, I might go without you.'

'When have you ever known me to be unpunctual?' Isobel bridled. 'A good nurse is always on time.'

'Who said you were a good nurse?' was his sardonic query.

Isobel had imperceptibly moved closer towards him at the door. She made a small grimace at his last remark.

'Miss Hilton, you might tell your brother that I'll be back by tomorrow afternoon, so don't let him go roaming around in my absence.'

'I'll pass on your instructions, Mr. Mallory,' she replied formally. If he was going to set this distant tone of 'Miss Hilton', then she would follow his lead.

'Good night,' he called. 'Come on, Isobel.' His arm went automatically around Isobel's waist and from the shelter of this half embrace, Isobel turned to say good night to Felicity.

Felicity waited only long enough to give the other two time to leave the villa. She did not want to appear that she was following them. As she went across the grounds towards the eye clinic where Trevor was staying, she wondered if Burne were staging a special show for her benefit. If he had heard that silly sentence about setting out to entrap him, he was obviously out to give her a lesson in how

74

difficult that task might be. If he had not heard, then making a show of taking Isobel to the mainland tomorrow was merely his way of equalising his favours to the available girls. One trip cancelled out another.

She told Trevor that Isobel and Burne Mallory were visiting the mainland next day. 'Anything you want—that is, that might be available?'

'Yes, boat magazines. Any that they have. Doesn't matter about the language. I can always get someone to translate. I need photos and diagrams.'

Felicity made a note of one or two other articles she wanted for herself, and later that evening slipped the envelope under Isobel's bedroom door, which was along the same corridor as Felicity's.

She was on her balcony where she had been reading for a while after she left Trevor and had just switched out the lamp on the little table when she heard a car drive up and stop outside the villa.

Peering cautiously over the rail she saw Isobel step out of Burne's car. Felicity turned away to go into her room, but angry voices below made her pause.

'What right have you to cut across my arrangements?' The voice sounded like Noel's. 'The moment you knew Isobel and I were going over to Monte Rubino, you had to interfere.'

Burne's reply was inaudible, but his mocking laughter was plain to hear. 'Sorry, old chap,' he said, 'but Isobel may prefer my more comfortable boat to the ferry.'

Felicity went into her room and quietly shut the french windows. She could open them later when the quarrel had ended. Burne, it seemed, delighted not only in beckoning the girls towards him, but also in baiting other men. Felicity felt sorry for Noel and wanted to show him that she was sympathetic towards him in his problem, but she could hardly pat him on the shoulder and tell him to cheer up.

A few days later she had occasion to visit one of the laboratories. He was seated in front of a row of test-tubes and when she entered he glanced up from his notes.

'Welcome!' he called. 'I've been doing these charts the whole blessed morning and I'm glad to see a visitor.'

She gave him the message from Dr. Johansen first and waited while he searched records, then wrote the required information on a printed form.

'Stay and talk to me for a while, if you have time,' he invited, pulling out a stool next to him.

'What shall we talk about?' she asked.

'Anything you like.'

'Then let's begin with my brother. Mr. Mallory is giving him treatment, but I expect you know that. Soon he thinks he may operate, unless he finds that not necessary.'

Noel moved a pile of charts out of his way, then turned towards her. 'Shall we try to leave Mallory out of the conversation. Professionally, he may be at the top of the tree, but personally the less I hear about him the better, and if he went out in his boat and it sprang a leak, I wouldn't shed a tear if he never came back.'

Felicity laughed gently at his vehemence. 'If he were in difficulties, you'd probably be one of the first to go out and rescue him.'

Noel shook his head. 'No fear!'

'But you'd never be able to forget that you're a doctor,' she continued.

'There are quite a few times when I come near to forgetting it,' he told her, 'I don't think I'd care so much if he'd have the decency to fight clean.'

'How d'you mean?'

'The way he picks up girls and then discards them. That's what I mean. If I thought for a moment that he really loved Isobel, then I'd say—"let the best man win"— and if she wanted me to clear out of the way, I'd go. But Mallory isn't made that way.' Noel swung round and stepped off his stool. With his hands in the pockets of his white coat, he began pacing up and down the small laboratory, three or four steps each way.

'Mallory has something wrong with him,' he went on,

almost oblivious now of Felicity's presence, except that she was the excuse of a sounding board. 'He's adolescent or still suffering from an inferiority complex and he can only bolster himself up by attracting every girl he claps eyes on.'

'Sooner or later he might meet one girl with whom he'll be satisfied,' put in Felicity, although she could not convince herself of this, let alone Noel.

'Then I hope to God he doesn't choose Isobel. She'll believe that he loves her, then when it suits him he'll break her heart.'

'But d'you know really what Isobel's feelings are towards him? She might really love him.'

Noel snorted angrily. 'At the moment she thinks she does. She knows that I love her, I've told her so enough times and meant it, but I'm too easy. Isobel doesn't mean to be cruel or unkind, but Mallory is more of a challenge to her. He plays hard-to-get and although she knows his reputation even here on this island, that appeals to her.'

'Many girls believe that they can reform a man if there is enough love between them,' Felicity observed.

Noel glared at her from under his dark, bushy eyebrows. 'Then I hope you can prevent yourself from such reforming zeal. You've seen for yourself that Mallory doesn't mind dallying a little of his time with you on one pretext or another. He always takes good care that Isobel knows about your outings in his boat. I suppose he thinks it keeps her jealousy nicely balanced. When she's ready to fly off the handle, oh, up he comes with a nice invitation to the mainland or something of the sort.'

'Well, at least I know that when he takes me out he's only amusing himself,' Felicity said calmly. 'I'd be a fool to think otherwise.'

Noel cast a sharp glance at her. 'D'you really think so? Or are you kidding yourself?'

'I'm twenty-four. I ought to have a bit of sense by now to know the difference.'

Noel laughed quietly. 'I wonder how many other girls

have said that and found afterwards that they were merely trying to convince themselves.'

'I thought we were trying to keep Mr. Mallory out of the conversation,' she reminded him. 'I really must go back to Dr. Johansen. He'll be sending out a search party for me.'

'Are you free tonight, Felicity?' Noel asked suddenly, as she walked towards the door.

'I spend most evenings with Trevor while he can't go out himself.'

'Then skip the boy for once and come down to the harbour with me. We'll go to *L'Aragosta* or Mariano's or anywhere you like.'

'Supposing Isobel is free and would like you to take her out?' she ventured.

Noel smiled bitterly. 'If she's free, she'd rather be with Mallory.'

'Don't you think that's where you make a mistake, Noel?' Felicity spoke firmly. 'You've got to fight for Isobel, if you want her, not let her go to another man by default. Assert yourself sometimes and you might be surprised by the results.'

'I've done that sometimes and the results have indeed surprised me, but not quite in the way you mean. My tactics have usually driven Isobel farther away than ever.'

'Look, Noel, tonight I'll come out with you for a stroll and a coffee or glass of wine, but only if Isobel is actually on duty. Otherwise, you can do your best to persuade her.'

Noel gave her a boyish smile. 'I like you, Felicity. You're refreshingly candid, but I should know, I expect, that candour goes with hair your colour.'

'The colour of my hair takes the blame for a load of mischief.' She waved a hand in goodbye and dashed back to her own office, hoping that her absence had not been too noticeable.

Dr. Johansen was not there and she put the record sheet on his desk, then went back to her own corner of the room.

'Oh, there you are!' She did not need to turn round to

78

know that the owner of the voice was not Dr. Johansen, but Burne Mallory.

'Did you want me?' she asked incautiously.

The long pause compelled her to turn towards him, for she thought he must have gone out of the room again.

His grey eyes were laughing at her. 'Want you? I'm not sure if I correctly understand your meaning.'

'Then was there some business point on which I could help you?' she said impatiently.

'That's better expressed. Actually, there is. I've decided to operate on your brother's eyes the day after tomorrow.'

'Then you've found out what was wrong?' she asked eagerly.

He sat in a chair opposite her. 'I can promise nothing. Not even that,' he said more gently than usual. 'I can say only that I *believe* I know the trouble and that if this operation does not completely cure, then it will at least not do any further damage to Trevor's sight.'

The eager light had died out of her eyes. 'I see.'

'Yes, and I hope to make you brother able to use those words "I see" just as carelessly as you do now. I need your written consent to the operation.' He took the form from his pocket and handed it to her for signature.

'I suppose it's not possible for you to tell me any details about what you're trying to do?'

'No. It's a fairly rare condition and doesn't conform to the more usual eye diseases. It's too technical for you to understand. I could discuss it only with someone else in my profession.'

She signed her consent and handed him the form.

'Thank you. Now I have a few instructions for you. You can look in on Trevor tonight for a few minutes, no more. Tomorrow he'll be isolated so that we'll prepare for the operation in the right conditions. He won't be alone. A nurse will be with him all the time. After the operation, I'll let you know when you can see him, but you'll understand that his eyes will be bandaged and he won't be able to see you.'

Felicity sighed. 'Yes, I understand. Trevor has been through all this before.'

'Not quite all,' Burne corrected her. 'Whatever other treatment he's had it is not the same as the operation I expect to perform.'

'Of course.'

'So the best thing you can do tonight is come out with me and take your mind off Trevor and his future.'

She stared at him. 'Thank you,' she answered with a smile, 'but you don't have to bother about me. I shall be all right and I shan't worry. As a matter of fact, I've promised to go out this evening with Noel.'

'Oh, indeed! I'm sorry if I appear to be competing for your company. By all means go with Noel. Have an enchanted evening.'

He rose and went from the room abruptly, leaving Felicity with a slight feeling of triumph. At last she had shown him that she could retain her independence, even in an approaching crisis. She began to giggle softly. How annoyed His Masterful Highness had appeared to be when she mentioned that she was going out with someone else! Perhaps if a few other girls had displayed a like independence, Burne Mallory might now be a more likeable and less conceited creature.

Felicity was quite proud of herself as she resumed her afternoon's work. It had not been too difficult after all to strike a blow for freedom and all that and chip a little of the clay under Burne Mallory's feet.

CHAPTER FIVE

WHEN she visited Trevor that evening for the few minutes' visit allowed, she asked the nurse first if he had been warned of his impending operation.

'Oh yes, he knows.'

He seemed cheerful enough and only too anxious for the days to pass so that he would have the bandages removed.

'It's rather a curse not to be able to look at those magazines Isobel brought back with her. They're full of boats of all sorts of shapes and designs.'

'A few more days, perhaps, and you'll be able to do all the looking you want to,' Felicity assured him, hoping that she was not raising his expectations too high.

He had been told that she would not be allowed in the clinic until at least one day after the operation, so he was apparently resigned to this.

'You know that the very moment I'm able to come, I shall be here, even if you can't then see me,' she said.

'Of course, Flissie. It's what I've come for, isn't it? Even if you have other ideas.'

She was puzzled a little by that remark, but forbore to ask for explanations. She did not want to worry him now on the eve of the most important ordeal he had been compelled to face.

When she left the clinic and returned to the villa she stood for a few moments in the vestibule. She had half expected Noel to be waiting for her, but no doubt some minor matter had delayed him. A quarter of an hour later one of the junior laboratory assistants brought her a note. She had barely time to open it and gather that Noel had taken her advice when Isobel came dashing down the stairs.

'Oh, hallo, Felicity! Have you seen Noel? I promised I'd go out with him tonight. I've refused him so many times that the poor darling is quite disconsolate, so I must cheer him up. If he comes here, will you tell him that I've gone to the main block?'

'Certainly. Enjoy yourself.' Felicity watched the other girl hurry across the courtyard and smiled to herself. Well, she had told Noel to try to take Isobel out unless the latter was on duty and evidently he had persuaded her. Now, in view of Isobel's flippant attitude, Felicity wondered whether she had done a wise, kind thing or the reverse. What would be the use if Noel's hopes were raised only to be dashed down again when Isobel was in a different mood?

She sat down on the vestibule bench. She would give Isobel and Noel a few minutes' start, then she would go down the road to the harbour, but she would take great care not to appear to be following them.

She picked up an Italian newspaper and tried to gather the gist of the news. After some twenty minutes she went outside the villa and there was Burne Mallory leaning against a stone pillar.

Felicity flicked her eyes away from him as he instantly straightened up and moved towards her.

'Don't tell me that Noel let you down!' he gibed.

'Not really,' she answered as calmly as she could. 'It was only a provisional arrangement that if we were both free, we'd——'

'Nonsense! He was running round in circles trying to find Isobel and see if she was off duty.'

'And apparently she was, so that's all right,' she said.

'Well, in that case——'

'Oh, please don't take pity on me,' she begged. 'I'm quite capable of walking down to the harbour for a breath of fresh air.'

'You shouldn't interrupt me, Felicity. How d'you know what I was going to suggest?' he demanded, his eyes alight with mischief.

'Only that you told me earlier today that I was to spend the evening with you if only to take my mind off Trevor.'

82

'I might have been inviting you to a game of snakes and ladders in the staff common room——'

'Very unlikely,' she snapped.

'You have that reproving look in your eye again,' he observed.

'Sorry, I'll blink it out.' But this was not the way to skirmish with Burne. A shuttlecock conversation would only end in defeat for her, she knew. She changed her tactics. 'If it's not seemly for me to go down to the harbour unescorted, I'll be glad of your company.'

He gave her a mocking bow. 'Thank you. Shall we go?'

But he did not take her towards the harbour. Outside the main gates of the clinic he turned his car towards the winding road that led uphill.

'Been up this way before?' he queried, as he negotiated a sharp bend.

'Only in the daytime.'

'The magic is lost in sunlight,' he said.

When he stopped the car she saw that they were in a small clearing. 'You have to walk from here,' he told her laconically.

Trust Burne to ruin her shoes, she thought resentfully. 'I'd have worn my brogues if I'd known,' she answered lightly.

But there was a well-defined path between clumps of bushes, then some stone steps. Enough daylight remained to enable Felicity to see the path, but now she thought it time to ask where it led.

'To a look-out that's been in use for a couple of thousand years or more,' he answered.

For the last few yards to the summit he grasped her hand and helped her to the little stone plateau edged by a wall. Below, the sea murmured against the rocks and when Felicity cautiously peered over the wall she saw that the cliff went sheer down to the sea.

'This was the point where in more troublous times they kept a sharp look-out for invaders,' he told her.

83

She could see the twinkling lights of the harbour, the fitful gleams from the other islands, Rondine and Lupa, and in the other direction, a cluster of pin-points defining the mainland.

'And now? Who looks for what?' she asked.

'Mostly the return of the fishing boats.'

'Or smugglers?'

He laughed. 'You've got smugglers on the brain, haven't you? Well, yes, I think it likely that in the past someone has shone a signalling light to some darkened little boat out there.'

'But not now? Has everyone reformed and left smuggling alone?'

'That's doubtful. Smuggling is always profitable to some people. Others welcome the danger involved.'

She wanted to ask him if that was the kind of danger that appealed to him, but thought better of it. Instead, she said, 'What made you say the magic of this place was lost in the sunlight?'

'Are you so insensitive, Felicity, that you don't feel the atmosphere of the place at night? Think of the treachery of those who gave false signals or those who crept up in the dark and tossed the watcher over that wall.'

'You make me shiver!' she protested.

'All right. Then think of all the romantic trysts and lovers' meetings up here,' he consoled her with a chuckle.

'Your imagination will soon turn that into a triangle with an angry husband thirsting for revenge.'

'Oh!' he exclaimed in mock horror. 'You're curdling my blood! Come, I'll have to take you away from this mysterious spot in case you disappear before my very eyes.'

She took a step or two away from the wall, then stopped.

'What's that noise down below? It sounded like a faint scream.'

'There are a dozen explanations, but all of them would frighten you. Actually, it's the wind blowing through a hole in the cliff.'

'How prosaic!' she mocked. 'I thought at least you'd spin a couple of yarns about that.'

He sighed loudly. 'We'll go down to the inn if that's prosaic enough for you.'

'An inn? Up here in this wild place?'

'You'll be surprised,' he warned her.

On the way down the path, he linked her arm tightly through his own so that she should not slip, but she neither pulled away from him nor leaned against him. It was not so easy, however, to feign the indifference that would have pleased her. She tried to imagine that he was no more than a brotherly companion, or even another girl more experienced in scrambling down rocky paths. But she was conscious of Burne's magnetism, his masculinity, his quick changes of mood that made her unsure that she could resist him.

In a sense she was both glad and sorry when they reached the car. At least he was occupied while he drove.

She was astonished when only a very short drive of no more than a few minutes brought them to the door of a small inn.

'Ah, I see. Handy refreshment place for the look-outs when they had finished their stint,' she said lightly.

Burne led her towards a garden at the side of the *taverna* where a couple of tables were placed under the trees. A plump young girl came to take Burne's orders and returned in a few minutes with an earthenware jug and two glasses.

'The wine will be good, but rough,' he told Felicity.

For some time they sat without speaking. Felicity was trying to assess this strange man who could be cynical and callous, then full of lighthearted teasing or coldly indifferent. Was this what had attracted so many other girls to him? She realised that not once during the evening had he spoken of Trevor, and for this she was immensely grateful.

From inside the inn came the sound of men's voices, then a burst of laughter followed by a small silence and the twang of a mandolin launching into a gay Neapolitan song.

85

After a few bars, men joined in with the words.

'D'you understand what they're singing?' she asked Burne.

'Oh, yes. It's a famous Neapolitan ditty, but——' He broke off, laughing. 'What they're singing is their own impolite version.'

'Just as well that my knowledge of Italian is not yet very far advanced,' she commented.

The mandolin-player began another tune, and now the company in the bar was hushed.

'No words to this one?' Felicity queried softly.

'Yes.' She glanced at Burne's face and in the dim reflection of light from the inn, she saw his features had become set and inexpressibly sad. Perhaps the melody aroused memories for him, memories that gave him no pleasure to recall. He was gently rotating the wine in his glass, his gaze fixed not on his present surroundings, but a different place and time that had risen before him in his mind's eye.

He set down his glass so violently that some of the wine spilled on the check tablecloth. 'Come on, Felicity. Time we went.'

He strode towards the inn door to pay for the wine. Two or three voices greeted him. Then as Burne turned away, replacing his wallet, a man came quickly out of the inn and spoke rapidly.

Burne waved him away and Felicity caught a few words that sounded like 'Not now, Luigi. Another time.' Her Italian was good enough to cope with simple phrases.

The man addressed as 'Luigi' shrugged and returned to the inn.

As Felicity and Burne walked towards the car parked a little distance along the road where it was wide enough to turn, the plangent yet sensuous sound of the mandolin followed, borne on the quiet, still air. She remained silent, aware that she had glimpsed a part of Burne's private world of torment that could be stirred by a sentimental tune. A month ago she would have been completely indifferent to his melancholy, but now she believed that underneath his veneer of conscienceless trifling lay a bitter, aching hurt, a constant legacy from his past.

In silence they entered the car and after what she judged as a suitable interval, Felicity said, 'That inn was an unexpected pleasure, tucked away like that, but then, I suppose, there are many others on the island, as well as the obvious ones down by the harbour?'

'A few,' he muttered. 'Wine, women and song. Italians don't take life more seriously than they need; at least, not in these parts. I don't blame them.'

She made no answer. She guessed that he was warning her not to take this evening's outing too seriously. It meant nothing but a visit to one of the island's romantic spots, and while he had spoken of magic in the atmosphere, he did not expect her to read into it anything more than an impersonal flavour.

Outside the villa she thanked him for taking her out. 'You were right,' she admitted, 'in helping me to take my mind off Trevor. Thank you—Burne.'

She hurried into the villa, her face flaming with colour. She had never called him 'Burne' before, even though she thought of him by his name. Would he now imagine that she was trying to follow up a fancied advantage in the hope of a mutual attraction?

It was easy enough to concentrate on her work next day, for this was only preparation day for Trevor. The following morning was harder to bear.

'You don't know what time Mr. Mallory is operating?' she asked Dr. Johansen.

'I don't know, but I think if I did I might not tell you,' he answered with a smile. 'You'd be watching the clock all the time and fretting about what was happening.'

'Yes, I expect so.' She finished the next report.

The doctor was gazing out of the window. Then he turned towards her. 'You said you'd never seen pomegranates growing. Would you like to tour some of the orchards to see the trees in flower?'

She was quick to respond to this sensible suggestion,

knowing that it was her chief's kindly way of lightening the tension she felt in connection with Trevor.

'I'd like that very much, if you could spare me.'

'We'll go together,' he offered to her surprise.

He gave a few instructions to his various members of staff and very soon he was driving up the hill and along the road where Burne had taken her last night. But Dr. Johansen took a different route and now the road led through orchards of small trees covered with brilliant flame flowers.

'Oh! What a lovely sight!' she exclaimed.

'You'll get a better view when we climb a little higher. Then from the car we can look down along the valley.'

'It's like seeing the Vale of Evesham in spring except that most of the blossom there is white or pink. But this— it's like a scarlet carpet.'

Dr. Johansen drove through a pair of wide open wooden gates and along a narrow track between columns of trees. A thick-set young man came towards them.

'*Ciao!*' he greeted the doctor, who replied the same way.

'This is one of the owners of a pomegranate orchard,' he explained to Felicity. 'Stefano Ramelli,' he introduced her, then added in Italian that Miss Hilton was his English assistant.

Felicity saw that this was no hard-pressed fruit-grower. He wore an immaculate cream silk shirt and his dark blue trousers were well cut. His wrist-watch on a gold mesh strap looked expensive and the sizeable diamond set in a ring on his little finger winked brightly in the sun.

But before any tour of inspection, first there was a short ceremony for a sip of maraschino in the shade outside a small hut.

'Now we start,' promised Stefano after the drinks had been lavishly handed round. He had enough English for Felicity to understand him, and in her turn, she tried a few phrases in Italian.

Stefano marched briskly in front along the rows, where men and women and sometimes small children worked with hoes under the trees. He explained that no metre of ground must be wasted on this tiny, rocky island, so vegetables were grown in the shade of the trees and thrived very well.

'Now you see why they called the island "Isola Rossa",' chipped in Dr. Johansen.

'From the sea it must look beautiful at this time of year,' observed Felicity.

'Then you must go to the other side to see it on fire,' explained Stefano. 'That is the way the land slopes.'

She made a mental note to ask Burne to take her that way soon, assuming, however, that he had a mind to invite her out in his boat.

'*Punica granatum,*' the doctor said. 'That's what the Romans called Pomegranates, but they were growing all round the Mediterranean even before then. In Caucasian districts parts of Afghanistan and so on they grew wild.'

'What are they called in Italian?' she asked.

'*Melagrane,*' replied Stefano. 'When the fruit is ripe, you shall have a large basket of our best quality, *signorina.*'

'*Grazie, signore,*' she thanked him.

Before she and Dr. Johansen left, Stefano gave them each a bottle of pomegranate juice.

'Ah! Last year's vintage,' commented the doctor. 'Was it a good one.'

'*Così, così,*' admitted Stefano. 'As you say, "So-so",' he added with a grin. 'This year will be better. Always we hope will be better.'

At the gate, a small girl clutching in her two fists a large bunch of the exquisite flame trumpets ran towards Felicity, curtsied and presented her with the bouquet.

'Today they are beautiful; tomorrow they will droop,' Stefano warned her. 'They do not last longer than a kiss.'

When Felicity and Dr. Johansen were in the car driving away, he said wistfully, 'Stefano is always the amiable host to visitors. I wish he could treat his workpeople as well.'

'Doesn't he pay them much?'

'No. Gradually he's bought up all the orchards on the island. He owns the lot, even though some properties are nominally in other names. He has a monopoly, and as pomegranates are the island's main source of trade most of the people depend on him for their livelihood.'

'He looks prosperous enough himself.'

'Oh yes,' agreed the doctor. 'He likes people to see that he can afford almost any kind of luxury.'

'Does he live here on Isola Rossa?'

'No, on the mainland. Oh, he has a wonderful villa, I'm told, along the coast near Monte Rubino. An apartment in Rome, a yacht in which he cruises around the Adriatic and the Greek islands. He comes here to Rossa only for very short visits—now when the pomegranates are in blossom, in September when the crop is exported, not many other times unless he has some big business deal on hand and wants to escape attention.'

Felicity laughed quietly. 'You sound as though you don't much care for Stefano Ramelli.'

He smiled. 'I'm not alone in that. He's probably the most unpopular man who ever steps ashore here.'

'Doesn't that make it dangerous for him? One dark night somebody might—perhaps——?' She left the sentence unfinished.

'I hope nothing like that ever happens to him. We don't want a *vendetta*. He has enemies, but he also has some very powerful friends.'

Felicity was silent. She wondered if perhaps even Dr. Johansen deemed it politic to keep on the right side of Stefano.

The name 'Stefano' jogged her memory of that day on Isola Rondine when Burne had greeted someone called 'Stefano' at the café. The name was common enough and she regretted now that she had not been curious, and perhaps ill-mannered, enough to turn her head to see Burne's acquaintance.

Dr. Johansen took her to lunch at the house of a friend. Evidently he had telephoned in advance before leaving the clinic, for the guests were welcomed enthusiastically. The hostess took charge of Felicity's flowers to put them in water in a cool corner, ice-cold drinks were served in a shady loggia, and the meal that followed was delicious. A clear soup in which floated thin slices of toast and tiny balls of *pasta* like china beads. Then the protracted dallying with artichokes resembling the blue-green of antique copper domes. Since coming to Italy Felicity had become acquainted with the leisurely stripping leaf by leaf, the tiny succulent morsel at the base of each, the butter sauce next to one's plate, finally the creamy, fleshy heart.

The main dish of grilled slices of beef with a green salad was followed by a soft cheese, crumbling and milky.

The end of the meal provided a surprise for Felicity, for instead of the maid who had served at table, a strikingly handsome girl brought in the coffee. Felicity started, for surely this was the girl whom Burne had met on Rondine coming up from the beach, the girl who had been embarrassed at meeting him again when her husband was so near at hand.

'My daughter, Emilia,' the hostess announced, banishing Felicity's further doubts, although only a socially polite smile crossed the girl's face. She gave no sign of recognition and Felicity took her cue similarly.

This was perhaps how Burne had come to know Emilia. Perhaps one day Dr. Hendrik Johansen had brought his colleague to visit this friendly family and Burne had seized the opportunity of what he had himself called 'a heady affair'. Perhaps it was an advantage that Emilia was now married and, one hoped, safe from Burne's attentions.

It was almost mid-afternoon when the doctor and Felicity said their final goodbyes to their charming hostess and her daughter. A roundabout route back to the clinic took up more time and on the way Dr. Johansen pointed out the ruins of a small church perched on top of cliffs.

'A commanding position, as you can see,' he observed, when he and Felicity walked over the rough tussocks of grass and weeds. 'The "wreckers'" church they called it, apparently. Lights were shown to misguide ships which then obligingly struck the rocks below. The wreckers were already down there, not to give any help, but to plunder

91

whatever they could find.'

'That sort of thing has happened in the past all round coasts, even in England.'

He nodded. 'All Scandinavia, too.'

'What happened to the church to make it a ruin?' she asked.

'There are legends about it, of course. Some say that on certain nights the ghostly figure of a girl appears, beckoning the seamen to their doom. Other versions deny the story and assert that the girl's lover was killed in one of these episodes, that she died of grief and that her spirit appears to warn ships and sailors to keep away. But the church fell into decay and, as you see, there's not much left of it now. There are two other churches in the town and this one was never particularly accessible.'

When he drove her back to the clinic she thanked him for an enjoyable day. 'It was thoughtful of you to arrange an outing so that I wouldn't be worrying about Trevor.'

His fair face crinkled into a smile as he looked down at her. 'Oh, I can't take that much credit. It was Burne Mallory who suggested it. I think I might have got around to it eventually, but he specially asked me last night.'

'Oh, I see. Well, anyway, thanks all the same.'

As she walked towards the villa she reflected that Burne could be considerate enough when he chose. Or was he trying to demonstrate that he had no objection if she went jaunting about with other men? She tried to stifle that last unworthy thought, which might be doing him less than justice. Because she did not understand him she told herself there was no need to impute the worst motives to him all the time.

At the foot of the stairs leading to her room she changed her mind. It was too early for dinner and she might as well use the time strolling about in the gardens and grounds.

She met Isobel near the main block and walked with her through the corridors.

'Had a good day?' asked Isobel. 'I heard you'd gone out with Hendrik.'

'Yes, I enjoyed it all very much. Tour of the pomegranate orchards, ruined churches, the lot.'

'I think there may be quite good news for you about Trevor,' murmured Isobel, lowering her voice, 'but don't count on it, and don't say I told you.'

Felicity's eyes shone. 'Oh, thank you, Isobel. I won't say a word until I'm told officially.'

'You can't see him tonight or possibly even tomorrow. Burne cloisters up his patients as well as himself for these operations. Also, he has a woman patient tomorrow. A very difficult case, I believe.'

After another remark or two, Isobel said, 'Must fly now. See you later.'

Felicity watched Isobel's slim figure in her white uniform disappear round the next corridor. In a sense she was a stranger in this atmosphere of specialist doctors and nurses, here almost on sufferance, useful only in her capacity as a competent typist and secretary. She was not even bilingual and still vaguely puzzled as to why Dr. Johansen had taken the trouble to bring her from London when no doubt English-speaking girls were more easily available in Rome or Milan.

She wandered out to the cloisters surrounding the inner courtyard of the main block. As Noel had said when she first arrived and as she had subsequently seen for herself, the shady cloisters provided excellent accommodation for patients at most stages of their treatment. In some cases, beds were wheeled out from the rooms behind, the former cells; those who were allowed to walk could stroll about or sit in the beautiful centre space where an ornate fountain played and splashed and numerous birds came to drink or bath themselves.

Noel had explained that when the building had been transformed from an almost abandoned monastery to a summer palace, many of the cell walls had been removed in order to make long, elegant salons.

'In some cases, we've had to replace more flimsy partitions for the sake of privacy,' he had pointed out. 'But all the cell doors, plain wooden slabs, were taken out and now you see these handsome full-length windows that lead directly on to the cloisters.'

Now as Felicity walked slowly across the courtyard, greeting first one patient, then another, she tried to imagine the gaieties, the balls, the amusements that had been seen here. A sharp contrast, no doubt, from the austere monastic round. Now the wheel had turned again and the monastery-palace had become a place of peace and healing.

A young nurse came towards her and told Felicity that she was wanted on the telephone. She took the call in Dr. Johansen's office.

Burne's voice came through rapidly. 'Not bad, I think. We can't be too certain of success, but we'll hope.'

'Any idea when I can see Trevor?' she asked.

'Not until tomorrow evening. I want him kept absolutely quiet. If he becomes restless and asks for you, I'll let you know.'

He had put down the telephone before she could even thank him.

The next day dragged itself out hour by hour until six o'clock when Felicity hurried to the eye clinic.

'Five minutes, please,' the nurse in charge warned her.

'Is that all?'

'*Sì, sì.*'

Burne was apparently elsewhere, but all Felicity's thoughts were concentrated on Trevor. His eyes were band-aged and his face looked unnaturally pale, but he sounded fairly cheerful.

'Has he made a job of it?' he asked Felicity. 'Or has he botched it?'

'You know he'd never botch it,' protested his sister. 'You have to wait and——'

'And see,' finished Trevor for her. 'That's what I hope.'

The five minutes flashed by, but in a sense Felicity was relieved at this stage not to stay longer, for Trevor's questions would have been too difficult for her to answer. She promised to come and see him again as soon as she was allowed to.

'There is one thing you could do for me, Flissie,' he whispered. 'While I'm cooped up here, I'm helpless.'

'Yes, what is it?'

'You know that Italian girl, Zia. You've met her a couple of times.'

'M'm.' Felicity hoped that Trevor's enforced stay in the clinic had banished thoughts of Zia from his mind.

'Well, I promised I'd let her know about a boat. She knows one or two men who might let me have one cheap— or hire one—and——'

'Look, Trevor, isn't it time to talk about boats when you're able to see well and then you can go down to the harbour and see for yourself what can be arranged?'

'Yes, but Zia won't know that I can't go down to the cafés or to her house. Could you take a message for me?'

Trevor's face was taking on an expression of anxiety and Burne had said that he must be kept absolutely quiet.

'*Signorina!*' called the nurse again.

Trevor clutched Felicity's hand. 'Go down tonight to Gino's and see if she's there——'

'Gino's!' exclaimed Felicity. 'I can't go there.'

'Oh, don't be so damned prissie!' he shouted back. 'No one will cut your throat. Oh, well, try Mariano's. He's respectable enough even for you, I should think. He always knows where everyone is and what they're doing. Leave a message with him that I'll——'

But now the nurse was adamant. 'Please, please!'

'All right, Trevor, I'll do my best,' promised Felicity as she was more or less forcibly removed from Trevor's room.

After dinner she decided that the sooner she went down to the harbour and returned the better it might be for everyone. But halfway down towards Mariano's, she still wondered if she were acting wisely. Burne had forbidden Trevor even to think about hiring boats until well after the operation because of the danger of a setback. Supposing her brother did lose this particular chance of a boat through the agency of Zia, would it matter very much?

On the other hand, Trevor would demand next time he saw her if she had given Zia the message and she could hardly lie to him.

By now she had reached Mariano's café. She would certainly not go to that night-club place called Gino's.

But for once Mariano was not helpful.

'Zia no come here,' he told Felicity. 'She like Gino's best.'

'Well, I don't want to go to Gino's looking for her. My brother wants to give her a message.'

Mariano stuck out his lower lip in a grimace. 'Zia not good girl.' He shook his head vehemently. 'No good for brother.'

Felicity smiled. Privately she shared Mariano's opinion, but this was too public a place to say so. 'It's only about a boat that Trevor wants to hire.'

'Still no good for boats,' persisted Mariano, handing Felicity her Martini.

'All right, it doesn't matter. If you should see her soon, will you tell her that my brother is having an operation on his eyes and can't come for at least a week.'

'I hope Zia do not come to my bar,' growled Mariano. 'If she come, I tell her.' He gave Felicity a sudden amiable smile. 'For your sake.'

There were only three or four men in the bar and Felicity drank her vermouth, thanked Mariano and moved towards the door. If she stayed any longer, one or other of the men would sidle over to her and offer his company.

As it was she had no sooner left Mariano's than one of the men came walking quickly behind her.

'*Buona sera, signorina,*' he greeted her.

When she had first come to Isola Rossa Felicity had not known how to rid herself of unwelcome attentions, even though each individual Italian might be charming. But having discussed the question with Isobel, she knew what to do.

'I am sorry,' she said in her now carefully practised Italian, 'but I have an appointment.'

The Italian beamed. 'That is good. But first I help you to find Zia Tonelli. I take you to Gino's?'

'No, thank you. It's not necessary.'

'But please, *signorina*. Gino's is a very nice place.'

Felicity shook her head. 'I told you. I have an appointment. I have to meet my lover.' This was the most effective way of ridding oneself of intruders, so Isobel had said.

'Is he handsome, your lover?' the man asked.

'Very handsome and very strong,' replied Felicity, beginning to enjoy a little embroidery. 'He must not see you with me or he will be very angry.'

'I can be angry, too.'

'Yes, but he is very big.' Somehow Isobel's advice did not seem to be taking effect. Felicity turned towards her companion. 'You understand? If he sees you, he will be very jealous.'

She swung round quickly and cannoned into someone coming down the harbour road.

'Oh, Burne!' she exclaimed. 'I'm sorry—I——'

The Italian glanced at Burne Mallory, muttered a couple of sentences and walked away smartly.

'What was all that about?' asked Burne. 'Was he a follower?'

Felicity burst into rather nervous laughter. 'A follower? You make it sound like a Victorian servant's young man.'

'So you were on your way to meet a lover?' he queried, laughter in his voice. 'Anyone I know?'

Although she knew he could not see that colour had flooded her face, she turned her head away. 'Well, that was only to get rid of him. But how did you know?'

'Perhaps you didn't catch his words or understand them. He said, "Oh, the English lover! Many girls hurry to meet him!"'

'And you recognised yourself at once?' She had begun to recover some of her poise.

'Naturally. Was it wrong?'

'How would I know? I haven't been here long enough.'

He took her arm. 'Then let that be a lesson to you not to

97

go roaming about the harbour cafés at night. Now that you've met this phantom lover, or at least a substitute for him, let's go down together and I'll guarantee that no Italian will follow you home. What were you doing down here in the first place, may I ask?'

He was propelling her back towards the way she had come.

'I—er—came down just for the sake of fresh air,' she said lamely.

'That's not quite the whole of it. That Italian also added before his hasty departure that he would give your message to Zia. Well?'

'Oh, it was just something that Trevor asked me to do.'

'Give his love to Zia, I suppose?'

'More or less. Oh, it's only a passing fancy he has and being cooped up for the time being, these things seem important.'

'I see.'

By now she and Burne were past Mariano's bar and nearing *L'Aragosta*. He said nothing more until he had found a table under the trees by the harbour wall.

'And what else were you to tell Zia if you found her?'

She did not answer for a moment or two. 'Is it really your concern?' she asked at last.

He lit his long, thin cigar. 'Probably it is. Anything about a boat?'

Felicity sighed. 'All that Trevor wanted was not to lose the chance of getting a boat through someone Zia knows. Now you have the whole story,' she ended with exasperation.

'Perhaps both you and Trevor may be glad in future that I have the whole story—if it is the lot,' he added with that doubtful tone he used so often. 'Zia is a very charming girl when she chooses, but it might be better for Trevor not to involve himself too deeply with her. As for a boat, he's not going to be in a fit state to go out in anyone's boat, his own or hired, for quite some time.'

She became silent. Then she asked stiffly, 'Does Trevor know that? You know how keen he is on sailing and motor-boats.'

'I know. Therefore it's your job to insist on his being more patient. I don't even know how successful this operation is going to be. Any kind of injury or shock is likely to have very disastrous effects.'

'I do see your point,' returned Felicity quietly. 'Of course you don't want all your good work to be undone because he's impatient to be up and about.'

After a long pause he asked, 'D'you want to dance?'

She shook her head. 'Not particularly.' She was content to sit here with Burne in the fairy-lit garden with the dark Adriatic stretching beyond the wall. Content even when he was in this didactic mood, admonishing her on her own impetuosity as well as Trevor's.

When they finally left *L'Aragosta* and the noisy music faded behind them, he paced slowly beside her up the hill to the clinic.

Along the dark private path leading through the grounds, he took her arm to prevent her from stumbling and near the main building, he swung her towards him.

'A pity you should be disappointed,' he said quietly. 'You were coming to meet your lover, you told that fellow down there. Then a phantom kiss from a phantom lover may not be very exciting, but it's all you'll get.' He took her faced in his two hands and planted a gentle kiss on her lips, then quickly released her. 'Good night.'

He left her to go to his own quarters and she walked towards the villa. On her balcony she sat for some time in the darkness, asking herself a few searching questions.

Tonight's charade had been amusing and Burne had taken it very well, even though he would have been justified in being angry and indignant, but would she now be happier if he were not a 'phantom lover' but a man who really loved her?

She understood only too clearly why girls must have flocked around him in the past. He was not unaware of his magnetic powers and he exploited them whenever it suited him.

It was doubly necessary, she told herself, to steel herself against him. She had no intention of falling in love with him, but there was always the danger that he might regard her opposition as a challenge to be overcome.

All the girls fell for Burne Mallory, so why not Felicity Hilton? Felicity would give him warm friendship, but no more.

CHAPTER SIX

It was more than a week later when Burne casually asked Felicity if she would like a trip to Monte Rubino one afternoon.

'I'm taking one of my patients to the mainland and picking up another,' he explained.

'Certainly I'd like to come if Dr. Hendrik can spare me.' She had adopted the casual habit of most of the staff in calling Dr. Johansen by his Christian name, although she usually added his 'Dr.' prefix.

'You're not indispensable, not even to Hendrik,' he mocked.

She knew that he often used his cabin-cruiser to collect patients from the mainland, for the comfortably upholstered bunks were useful and the patients completely protected from the weather. Usually one of the nurses accompanied him, and today was apparently no exception, for Luella, who lived at the villa, was on 'cabin-cruiser' duty.

Felicity wondered why Burne had invited her as well as Luella who was obviously essential, whereas Felicity was only out for the ride.

The little town of Monte Rubino seemed to be preparing for a fête or gala occasion. The streets were beflagged and partly decorated with coloured lights. The cluster of shops by the harbour had their upper floors decked with flowers and window-boxes.

'A festival coming along?' enquired Felicity when she stepped ashore.

'Opening a new Casino,' Burne told her. 'I'll have to tell you about it later.' He and Luella helped the woman he had brought from the clinic to a waiting car, where she was enthusiastically greeted by relatives, who patted Burne on the back excitedly. So evidently that operation was an

101

entire success.

The car drove away and Burne and Luella looked about expectantly. After a while he said, 'Well, they don't seem to have turned up. So we'll use a little time in the café opposite.'

Over coffee and pastries Burne pointed out the dazzling white building near the shore, but a little distance from the harbour. 'The new Casino, built with ill-gotten gains and the promise of parting fools from most of their money.'

Luella looked at him with enquiring eyes and he translated for her benefit.

'Have they an old Casino then where they are generous to the fools and give them their money back?' asked Felicity.

Burne laughed. 'Casinos are run for profit, as you should know. Yes, there's a small old one, but the roof falls in whenever there's heavy rain and naturally the gamblers believe it spoils their luck.'

Felicity laughed disbelievingly.

'Actually some of us have been invited to the Grand Ceremonial Opening,' Burne continued. 'Want to come?'

'When is it?'

'Day after tomorrow.'

She considered for a moment, wondering if Trevor would be allowed to come too.

'No, I'm afraid not,' Burne answered in reply to her question. 'Your brother is not yet equal to night trips by sea. Another time.' He turned towards Luella, who accepted eagerly, providing she was off duty that night.

So it was to be a small party, not just Felicity and Burne.

'I'd like to come very much. Who else will be invited?'

'Oh, Isobel. Hendrik if he cares to join us. I'll bring as many as the boat will hold,' Burne promised.

He rose quickly. 'I think our new patient has arrived. Will you come, Luella?' He put down some money on the table and hurried off, leaving Felicity to finish her coffee.

Two other nurses alighted from the car which had drawn up at the quayside and Felicity watched while the woman was lifted out, placed on a stretcher and carried to Burne's cabin-cruiser.

Even now Felicity thought it remarkable that patients with serious eye diseases should undertake long and sometimes uncomfortable journeys to be shipped off to a remote island where they hoped to be cured. Yet Burne's reputation must be such that the journey became an unimportant detail.

At first she had assumed that only comparatively wealthy people could afford to come to Mr. Mallory on Isola Rossa, but Hendrik had told her that Burne made no distinction between rich and poor. He would operate on a penniless boy just as readily as on the daughter of a Milan millionaire and adjust his fees accordingly.

'Sometimes he will work without a fee at all, even give money out of his own pocket to help his patients after they leave here,' Hendrik had added. 'Of course he can pick and choose his cases. Every day a new list comes in, but he has to fix a limit.'

Felicity realised how lucky she and Trevor both were in hearing, if indirectly, of so accomplished a surgeon. The subject of fees had never yet been mentioned in connection with Trevor and this was something that Felicity thought might be more delicately dealt with through Dr. Hendrik when the time came for discussion.

Burne now signalled to her that he was ready to leave and she walked from the café to the quayside, jumped into *La Perla* and was astonished to find that Isobel was aboard.

'I came over earlier in the day,' she explained, 'but as Burne's boat happened to be here, I thought I'd thumb a ride home.'

After a few moments Isobel asked, 'Did Burne tell you we're all going to the Casino opening?'

'Yes, he did. I'm not sure if I ought to leave Trevor and go off gallivanting.'

'D'you think he'd stay behind if you were ill?' Isobel asked.

'Of course he would, if necessary.' Felicity's loyalty was not to be shaken in spite of Isobel's sceptical smile.

103

Hendrik later that day said he might not make one of Burne's party. 'If I can't go, I'll hand my invitation on to someone else.'

'Oh, then we have special invitations to the Casino?' queried Felicity.

'Certainly. Stefano Ramelli—the orchard-owner you met the other day—I understand he's put up a good deal of the money for the Casino, so he's given the clinic staff a lavish number of gilt-edged cards. I believe you get free chips for stake money, too.'

'Then if you can spare me I'd certainly like to go,' she decided. 'What an experience to gamble mildly with the Casino's money and not your own!'

Burne's boat *La Perla* was filled to capacity when he took his party to Monte Rubino. Luella had a couple of escorts, young laboratory assistants, Hendrik had managed to come and was talking earnestly to Isobel. Several others of the clinic staff whom Felicity knew slightly had also taken the opportunity of transport to a jollification.

Burne had impressed on Felicity the hazard of being lost in the crowds and when she had been ashore in the little gaily decorated town she realised how easy that was. Prudently she kept close to Isobel or Hendrik, not wishing exactly to hang on Burne's arm.

The Casino was not due to open officially until ten o'clock, but the guests could enter at nine. Before then, while daylight still lasted, there were preliminary gaieties. Processions with bands, children carrying flowers, grotesque gigantic figures with terrifying masks.

'We ought to be down by the shore at eight o'clock,' Burne told Felicity. 'There's a special "happening", so I'm told.'

'What sort of "happening"?'

He grinned at her. 'Don't spoil my fun and your own by being so inquisitive. Wait and see.'

Along the quayside were stalls selling balloons and pastries, toy models of the Casino and glasses of wine, souvenirs of Monte Rubino, plates of fish, everything.

She was eating small shellfish at a stall and watching a pageant of performers in medieval costumes. Hendrik tapped her arm. 'At eight o'clock we are ordered to see an exhibition,' he said. 'Come now.'

A sandy beach had been cleared and was now surrounded by a fringe of spectators. Somewhere in the town a church clock chimed and began eight strokes, other bells joined in and on the shore the sense of expectancy deepened. People raised binoculars, passed them to their companions. Then suddenly there was a shout of 'Here they come!' mingled with cries of '*Ecco!*' and wild Italian shouts.

Slowly three little ships approached, sails filled, manned by men stripped to the waist and rowing like galley-slaves.

The entire beach was deserted except for the spectators. The ships beached themselves and now the crews leapt ashore, brandishing knives and clubs. Suddenly from hiding places behind boulders or shrubs the defending warriors stepped out and gave battle to the attacking pirates.

Dead and injured bodies littered the sand until only half a dozen valiant fighters were left. Finally, the victorious islanders pushed the invaders into the sea, where three of them clambered into one boat and rowed away as fast as they could.

Triumphant shouts now rang out from the battle leader, all the dead and injured rose and capered about, embracing and fraternising with each other, pirates and islanders alike, before moving away to a temporary bar that had been set up to provide them with refreshment.

Felicity was still laughing when Hendrik called to her as the crowds were moving away in search of further spectacles.

'I've never seen anything so amusing,' she said. 'How different history might have been if all the pirates had agreed to appear at eight o'clock sharp! Think of it, Hendrik. All those Danes marauding our coasts and after them, the Jutes, Angles, Saxons, to say nothing of the Normans.'

'Think how uncivilised you might still be in your little

islands,' he retorted. 'Even the Romans left you with excellent roads. Baths, too.'

She laughed. 'Probably the Britons didn't know what to do with baths, any more than they did with the villas and mosaic pavements.'

Isobel and Burne were some little distance ahead. When Felicity looked again, the pair in front had disappeared.

The new Casino was a long, low building of dazzling whiteness illuminated now by floodlights. Hendrik and Felicity stepped through the portico entrance and found themselves almost enveloped in the crush of chattering people inside. Eventually they extricated themselves and found more space in the dance and dining salon that overlooked the sea. Hendrik miraculously whisked a couple of drinks from a passing waiter with a tray and almost immediately Stefano appeared, very smart tonight in formal evening dress.

'You like our new place?' he enquired of Hendrik.

'Yes. What I can see of it,' was Hendrik's cautious reply.

'Soon we open the rooms with the tables,' Stefano promised. 'I hope you win.' He marched away to talk to other guests.

'I suppose he's so rich he doesn't know what to do with his money,' hazarded Felicity.

'He's not exactly pouring it down the drain here. Most Casinos are profit-making concerns.'

Punctually at ten o'clock there were first calls for silence, then a short speech by Stefano, followed by the ceremonial opening with a golden key of the gaming rooms. This latter task was performed by a pretty Italian girl wearing a long, clinging ruby satin dress.

'Oh, of course!' murmured Felicity. 'A compliment to Monte Rubino, the Ruby Mountain. Did anyone ever find rubies here?'

'I don't think so. Only paper lire and lots of it, they hope.' Hendrik was surveying the crowd that eagerly trooped into the roulette and other rooms. 'I haven't seen

Isobel here. Have you?'

'No, not yet.' Felicity remembered that she had not seen Burne either since the end of the mock pirate landing.

'Well, we may as well use our lucky chips,' Hendrik suggested after a while. 'How good a gambler are you?'

Felicity laughed. 'I don't know. I've never been in a Casino before or played roulette, but I never have any luck in a Derby sweepstake.'

'All the better for you.'

Together they pushed their way into the large gaming salon and approached a table where players encircled it four or five deep.

'Could I watch first what goes on?' asked Felicity.

'If you can see over the heads or between all this crush.'

But she was hardly wiser for watching. The mysteries of red and black, odd and even, still baffled her. A group of players in front of Hendrik suddenly left, bemoaning that their free supply of stake chips had run out. Hendrik instructed Felicity where to place her stakes and when she did exactly the same as he, she won. After a few spins of the wheel she decided to be independent. Now she lost consistently until her last chips had gone.

Hendrik grinned at her. 'Always give up when you're losing. You'll never get back your winnings.' He rose from the table, giving place to others.

'I've heard that you should always stop when you're winning, too,' she said, as they walked away.

'Perhaps one should never begin. Then you would never know what your luck was like.' He sounded depressed, and for the second time this evening she wondered if he were alluding to the old saying 'Lucky at cards, unlucky in love'.

He went to the desk to change his counters into cash and at that moment she saw Burne and Isobel only a yard away.

'Well?' he asked Felicity. 'How did you gamble?'

'I lost. Hendrik won.'

'That was to be expected. I can't think for the life of me

why Hendrik doesn't turn into a professional gambler. He has the luck of the devil. He'd break any bank, even Monte Carlo.'

'Perhaps gambling doesn't appeal to him all that much,' remarked Felicity, eyeing once again Isobel's white dress heavily embroidered at neck and waist with multi-coloured sequins.

'Poor Hendrik,' murmured Isobel. 'Here he comes. You'd never believe he'd won anything, would you? He looks as though he hasn't even his return fare to Paris.'

'Casinos always give you a return fare to most places,' Burne reminded her. 'They don't like you to end up dying on a stone bench in the beautiful grounds outside.'

'Who's going to die on a stone bench?' asked Hendrik, near enough to have heard that last remark.

'You, if you don't leave the temptations of roulette and baccarat behind you,' answered Burne with a wide grin. 'Come on, let's go and eat. Is this place geared up for dinner, do you think?'

'Not tonight, I should say,' Hendrik replied. 'Stefano has been too busy organising the rest of the place.'

A few people were scattered at the tables surrounding the dance floor, but Burne and Hendrik decided that good service could hardly be expected on this first night.

'We'll go to a place I know where they have a roof restaurant,' suggested Burne. 'Then we can watch the fire-works.'

He led the way up a couple of back streets, down an alley and through a gate that opened on to another street. An outside staircase gave access to a small restaurant on the roof, partly covered by awnings.

'I didn't know this place existed,' confessed Hendrik.

Burne's gentle smile indicated that he would not expect Hendrik to know.

'Oh, I've been here several times,' commented Isobel. 'With Burne, of course.' She gave Hendrik a slightly pro-vocative glance and now for the first time it dawned on Felicity that Hendrik was very much in love with Isobel,

108

while she, in her turn, had only eyes for Burne.

How galling it must be, she thought, for Hendrik to be compelled to watch Burne playing fast and loose with Isobel! Or was Burne in earnest this time and willing to give all his devotion to her? Then where did Noel Bennett come in? He, too, was wildly infatuated with the attractive Isobel. Felicity decided in her mind that poor Noel stood no chance at all between these other two contenders, Burne and Hendrik. She was fortunate in that she could stand at the ringside as a watcher and was not involved herself. There were times, of course, when she had come dangerously close to being drawn towards Burne, but happily she had always had the good sense to react before any possible damage could be done. It was a little consoling to feel that she had retained that independence and freedom of affections that she had determined on when she had first known Burne and his widespread favours.

'Felicity! Wake up!' prompted Isobel. 'Burne is asking what you would like to eat?'

She gave herself a slight shake. 'Oh, sorry. I was dreaming.'

'A rhapsody on a bed of roses, by the look on your face,' commented Burne, and she winced at the savagery in his voice. What right had he to criticise her dreams when they were known only to herself?

She bent her head to the hand-written menu, for the restaurant offered only a limited number of dishes, but when the food came it was so delicious that she enjoyed it, in spite of having been nibbling at something or other most of the evening.

Small lanterns on iron posts were the only illumination up here on the roof and from here there was a wonderful view of the town below with its harbour, the bay beyond and the dim outline of mountains farther away.

Felicity had never seen such extravagant and colourful fireworks. On top of the Casino's white dome set pieces were illuminated at intervals, rockets soared into the blue-black sky to burst into showers of pink rain or green stars.

From a boat anchored in the bay a series of catherine wheels maintained a constant display and from the rocks close by the shore jumping streams of green or yellow light leapt like flying fishes.

Felicity clasped her hands in almost childish wonderment. 'It's like all the Guy Fawkes nights I've ever known rolled into one,' she exclaimed. 'Better, in fact. More colour.'

'Imagine what trouble Stefano has gone to,' said Burne. 'The expense—the work. At least one person is pleased.'

Her eyes still on the flashing lights around her, she did not reply. 'Stefano can no doubt afford it,' she said after a pause. 'Isn't that so, Hendrik?'

But Hendrik was not there. Nor was Isobel. Felicity was alone with Burne.

'Oh! Have the others gone?'

'Yes,' he answered softly. 'They thought it was time to be getting back to the boat. It's past midnight.'

'But why didn't you——' she began.

He put a firm hand on her shoulder. 'You were so entranced by the fireworks that it seemed a shame to drag you away.'

'Well, we have to go some time. We might as well go now.' She stood up, then fumbled for the lacy wool stole that she had brought with her. Burne picked it up from the floor. He draped it around her shoulders and before she could prevent him, he turned her swiftly towards him and kissed her.

'Oh, I see,' she said tartly. 'Another phantom kiss from a phantom lover!' Then she saw that was a fatal thing to say. She wished she had the power to unsay the words.

'Phantom?' he mocked lazily, but fortunately for her, the *padrone* of the restaurant came forward with Burne's change from the bill and was asking volubly if everything was all right.

'*Si, si, molto bene,*' replied Burne brusquely.

Felicity went down the outside staircase and the sudden flash of light from yet another firework shone on the house

110

opposite. On a similar outside staircase stood a young girl, dark-haired and smiling. She was leaning over the balcony rail and raised her hand in greeting, but Felicity was uncertain whether the gesture was meant for her or for Burne who was close behind.

'What's biting you?' Burne asked after they had walked through several streets in silence.

'Nothing much, except that I'd rather not be treated like a child,' she answered mildly.

'And were you? When?'

'You could easily have told me that the others, Hendrik and Isobel, were leaving, couldn't you?'

'Are you sore because Hendrik changed his partner?'

'No, of course not,' she snapped. 'We weren't tied together.' After a moment she added, 'Perhaps I'm surprised that you allowed Hendrik to go off with Isobel.'

'Perhaps I engineered the whole thing just that way,' he retorted. 'Flattered?'

'Not particularly.'

'All right. I'll remember next time—if there *is* a next time,' he threatened.

Along the quayside there were still plenty of merrymakers, laughing and singing and Burne guided her carefully out of their more boisterous path.

'Hendrik's in love with Isobel, isn't he?' she said suddenly.

'Is that a statement or a question?'

'An observation, perhaps.'

'Then I can't say whether your perceptions are accurate or not,' he answered gravely. 'How would I know?'

She wanted to assert that if Burne left Isobel alone, then Hendrik might have a chance. Instead, she muttered, 'Oh, it was just a feeling I had. Hendrik's tone of voice when he speaks to her—that sort of thing.'

'Flimsy evidence,' he scolded. 'You can't go round making accusations like that. Actually, if it will put your mind at rest, I might tell you that it's quite possible that Hendrik does at the moment believe he's in love with Isobel.'

111

'Why only "believe"?' she queried.

'Because Hendrik is much more in love with his work and his ideals than he could possibly be with any woman. There are times when he thinks he's missing something in life and he toys with the idea of marriage. He's thirty-five and sometimes it crosses his mind that he ought to settle down with a wife and raise a family. So he comes out of his shell, looks around, finds an attractive girl—imagines she might be the one. Then—bang!—back he scuttles into the security of his work. He feels safe there.'

'You make him sound a very cold fish,' she objected.

'Indeed, no. On the contrary. If he really were a cold fish, he'd make a survey of the likely partners, marry one of them, whichever was the most willing, and that would be that, without emotional splendour or anything else.'

By now they had arrived at the spot where Burne's boat was tied up, so Felicity had no chance to ask further questions that might have enabled her to discover whether that was the way Burne, too, looked at marriage. As a mundane partnership? But Burne and Hendrik were two entirely different types of men. They might eventually go through life as bachelors, but for quite opposite reasons.

Even though she and Burne had arrived back late, Luella and one of her escorts were still missing.

'I've a good mind to leave them here,' murmured Burne after some minutes.

'What's the hurry?' queried Isobel. 'Can it be that you've forgotten what it's like to be young?'

'Perhaps I never had the advantage of knowing,' he retorted, bending down to her with a mocking grimace.

Hendrik, seated next to Isobel, laughed. 'Coming from you, Burne, that sounds quite false. Completely untrue.'

'Ah, yes,' continued Isobel. 'Always the young in heart, that's Burne.'

Felicity detected a rather acid note in Isobel's voice. Was she annoyed at having left Burne at the restaurant with Felicity?

Eventually someone spotted Luella and her companion

112

mooning along the quayside at a dreamy pace. Shouts and laughter greeted the pair when they clambered aboard, but Luella was in no way abashed.

Burne cast off and *La Perla* glided out of the harbour and across the dark water. Someone started a song, the others joined in. Rollicking Neapolitan tunes followed by wistful love songs. Far away, another homegoing boatload laughed and sang, snatches of tunes echoed across the water.

Something caught and tore at Felicity's throat, a poignancy composed of the evening excitements followed by this calm idyllic ending. In two or three short months' time she would be back in England. Trevor would be cured and able to think about some employment. But this night would remain in her memory, a night when she had discovered not only how elusive one man could be, but the fact that Burne Mallory's inconstancy had the power to undermine that vaunted independence of heart of which she had been so proud. He had penetrated her carefully built defences and she had become just like all those other girls, ready enough to throw herself at him. But she would never yield to these weaknesses. She would build up anew those crumbling defences, be grateful for all he had done for her brother and leave Isola Rossa as heart-whole as she had arrived.

La Perla joggled gently against the harbour wall and the occupants made ready to climb out.

Burne, standing on shore, took her hand, then lifted her bodily on to the ground. Her new resolutions vanished like a pricked bubble and she moved away from him as though he were a flame and she was in mortal danger of being scorched.

She was glad to sit in the back of Hendrik's car with Luella and the young laboratory assistant, while Isobei sat in front with Hendrik. What a blessing that Burne had stayed behind to attend to his boat! Tomorrow Felicity would really get a grip on herself and not be swayed by silly romantic notions after an evening's entertainment.

113

CHAPTER SEVEN

THE day after the Casino opening was a busy one for Felicity. There were numerous reports to be typed, files to be checked and records to be indexed and kept up to date.

'No more gallivanting for a while,' she remarked to Hendrik.

'A little gallivanting does everyone some good,' he replied.

Trevor was now allowed to walk in the gardens for a short time each day and he began to chafe at his enforced idleness.

Burne had indicated that the boy might soon be well enough to go on longer walks, but not unaccompanied.

'He needs constant care for a while,' Burne had warned Felicity. 'You must impress on him the need for going steady. Otherwise, all my work is undone. The slightest blow or knock on the head—and I can't be responsible for the consequences.'

Felicity now spent all her evening free time with her brother, sometimes reading to him or they played cards, but he was moody and restless.

'When can I go out like a human being?' he demanded.

'If you'll only be patient for a little longer,' begged Felicity, 'you'll be able to go everywhere soon.'

Two days later a nurse mentioned to Felicity that Trevor had not returned from his morning stroll, nor had he come in to lunch.

Felicity thanked her and went in search of Hendrik. 'I can make up the time later on with your work,' she offered, 'if you'll give me permission to go and look for Trevor.'

'Any idea where he might be?' asked Hendrik.

Felicity's mouth was grim. 'Only one place. At the harbour.'

Noel gave her a lift down to the harbour, for he was on his way to another part of the island.

At first Felicity could not see Trevor anywhere. She called in at Mariano's bar and asked if he had seen her brother.

Mariano laughed. 'Oh, he is asking to be robbed. He wishes to buy a boat, he says.'

'*Buy* a boat?' exclaimed Felicity, horrified. 'He hasn't the money for that. I thought he wanted to hire one.'

'*Signorina*, come with me.' Mariano's portly figure accompanied her to the door of his bar. He pointed to the far side of the harbour. 'Go quickly. He is with Tomaso and Fortunato and they will try to sell him a boat with holes in.'

'Oh no, I hope not. In any case, he can't possibly buy anything.'

She found Trevor and the two Italians below the harbour wall, all three sitting on a flight of stone steps. A small decrepit-looking boat bobbed at her mooring.

'Hallo, Trevor!' Felicity called. He flushed and glanced guiltily away. Tomaso and Fortunato called '*Buon giorno!*' and smiled.

She walked down the steps and sat above the three men.

'What goes on?' she asked.

'I'm negotiating for the boat,' admitted Trevor.

'Buying or hiring?'

'Well, as a matter of fact, I thought if I could buy it cheaply, it might be less expensive than hiring.'

'Whose money is going to pay for it?' she demanded quietly. She did not want to embarrass her brother too much in front of Tomaso who understood English fairly well.

Trevor laughed. 'I only want a loan for the time being.'

'I see. How much is the boat?' she asked.

'Tomaso wants forty-five thousand lire. I know it sounds terrific in lire, but it's really less than thirty pounds.'

'It seems reasonable,' replied Felicity, who knew less

115

than nothing about the price of boats, but even she suspected that the price was too cheap for a sound dinghy. 'Is the engine included?'

'Oh yes,' agreed Trevor. 'That's what makes it such a bargain.'

'Then could we go for a trial run? You always do that if you buy a car, so that must also be right for a boat.'

Trevor hesitated and cast a sidelong glance at Tomaso. 'As a matter of fact, I've already been out in her,' he admitted after a pause. 'She's all right.'

'Very good boat,' interposed Tomaso.

'No leaks?'

Tomaso appeared shocked by the very suggestion of unseaworthiness. 'No leaks. Good engine. She goes like the wind.'

'And that's another thing,' chimed in Trevor. 'I can also use her for sailing.'

'Of course,' agreed Felicity. 'You've always been more keen on sailing than on boats with engines, haven't you?'

'Then it's agreed?' he asked eagerly. 'I can make the deal?'

'Not yet,' replied Felicity. 'I think we should take a day or two to think over the proposition. Let's say we'll come down on Thursday and decide finally.'

'But, Flissie!' protested Trevor. 'In the meantime it may be sold. Tomaso has other offers. I'll never get a bargain again like this.'

She turned to Tomaso. 'Surely you can hold it for two days for my brother? Only two days.' She wanted to delay matters so that if possible someone else could inspect the shabby-looking boat. Burne, Noel, even one of Luella's men friends, would probably glance at it and test the engine.

'Oh, really!' cried Trevor disgustedly. 'I'd have had the whole thing signed and settled if you hadn't come along interfering.'

Felicity merely smiled, forbearing to point out that preventing a hasty decision was the purpose of her interference. She rose to go up the steps. 'Coming, Trevor?'

A smart, freshly painted dinghy was approaching the steps. A youth in a blue shirt and jeans shut off the engine and veered the boat to the steps to allow a man in fawn-coloured jacket and trousers to alight.

Felicity saw that the newcomer was Stefano Ramelli. '*Signorina!* A pleasant surprise!' he greeted her.

Tomaso and Fortunato scurried up the steps while she introduced Stefano to Trevor.

After a moment's conversation, Felicity explained that her brother wanted a boat, but she thought it more cautious to wait for more expert advice.

Stefano listened carefully. 'I can make you much better offer,' he said breezily. 'For thirty thousand lire you can have one of my boats, very good, very strong. Then when you leave you can sell it back to me. Who tries to sell you this old wreck?' He pointed contemptuously to the boat belonging to Tomaso. Then he nodded. 'Ah, it was Tomaso, the wretch.'

Felicity said nothing, not wishing to make an enemy of Tomaso, but Trevor said, 'Tomaso's boat didn't seem too bad to me, except it wants painting.'

Stefano was now at the top of the steps with Felicity and her brother. 'Do nothing until you have seen the boat I offer you. Come with me.'

He shepherded the pair to the little bathing beach past the harbour. There drawn up beside the wooden staging was a sturdy dinghy, well painted, her outboard motor lying neatly against the thwart, a sail rolled up and stowed along the bottom-boards. The name *Violetta* appeared on the bows.

'There! Magnificent?' queried Stefano.

Trevor's face was all smiles and no doubt behind his dark glasses his eyes were shining. 'Magnificent indeed!'

'Now you can have your friends, perhaps the nice Doctor Johansen or anyone else, come and take out *Violetta* and test. Is it fair offer?'

'Very fair indeed,' conceded Felicity. 'Thank you, Signor Ramelli. We'll certainly consider it all very carefully.'

117

'Why not snap it up today?' protested Trevor.

'No, no, no!' cried Stefano. 'You must take time. She will be here for a few days. No hurry. I promise not to sell to anyone else.'

He escorted Felicity and Trevor back towards the harbour and suggested coffee at *L'Aragosta*.

'We're probably taking up your time,' Felicity said diffidently.

'No, no. There is always time for pleasant company,' he returned gallantly.

She thanked him for the invitation to the Casino opening and said how much she had enjoyed everything.

'You win at Casino?' he asked, his white teeth flashing in a dazzling smile.

She laughed. 'No, I lost all my free counters. Then I packed up. I mean I stopped,' she added, seeing his puzzled frown.

She gazed out at the shimmering sea and noticed a large luxury yacht moored a little way out.

'It is mine!' Stefano admitted proudly, seeing her questioning glance.

'There's a beauty for you,' whispered Trevor, reverence in his voice. 'What wouldn't I give for a trip in her?'

'Perhaps one day I take you—and your beautiful sister—for a cruise?'

Felicity smiled politely. 'That would be nice, but I also have to work here. Will you excuse us, Signor Ramelli? We'll let you know about the dinghy.'

When she and Trevor walked back along by the harbour they met Tomaso and Fortunato. The pair seemed to be arguing and Felicity wanted to steer clear of the two Italians, but Trevor went up to them and tried to apologise in English.

'What's Italian for "I'm sorry"?' he called to Felicity.

'*Mi dispiace*,' she answered, following Trevor.

Tomaso shrugged. '*Non importa*. Do not matter.'

Felicity smiled. 'You say "*Doesn't* matter" in English,' she corrected him, adding her apologies in her best Italian, but reminding him that her brother had not yet bought any boat, but was only considering Signor Ramelli's offer.

'Forto always unlucky,' remarked Tomaso. 'Hoodoo.'

Felicity laughed. 'You mean he puts a jinx on things?'

Tomaso nodded, then laughed too. He was not the type to be downcast for long, but Fortunato wore his usual melancholy expression.

When Felicity and Trevor were on their way back to the clinic, Trevor said, 'Perhaps that was a stroke of luck, Stefano Ramelli turning up like that. I might easily have settled for that old hulk that Tomaso was offering.'

'I hope you wouldn't have settled for anything without properly testing it out. We shall have to take advice about the other boat, the *Violetta*. Hendrik, perhaps, might help us, especially as he knows Stefano well.'

But Hendrik declared that boats were not really in his line. 'Of course, I can tell whether it is a good boat or a bad boat if it starts to sink, but Burne is the man you want. He's quite expert, I believe. He seems to handle his own cabin-cruiser very well.'

Felicity had been trying to avoid asking Burne for his assistance, but on reflection she saw that it might be safer to let him know that Trevor was madly keen to get hold of a boat of some sort.

'You must have made a remarkably good impression on Stefano,' was Burne's immediate reaction when Felicity told him the price.

'Is it—cheap?'

His jaw dropped ludicrously and his eyes goggled. 'Cheap! Unless it's a child's toy boat, he's practically giving it to you. It's those blue eyes of yours that bowled Stefano over.'

'I was wearing my sun-glasses anyway, so I don't suppose he could see the colour of my eyes.'

Burne sighed dramatically. 'All right, I'll put the dinghy through its paces for you. Even at the price you could still be robbed if the engine won't go or half the Adriatic comes in.'

119

'When?' asked Trevor, unable to curb his impatience.

Burne turned his head slowly towards the boy. 'I don't think I should really encourage you to take risks careering about in boats, but I've come to the conclusion that you're determined to go sailing, with or without my consent. So you might as well have a boat that can be trusted instead of going in someone else's unseaworthy job.'

'Thanks a lot,' was Trevor's quick response. 'I'll be terribly careful not to bump my head or anything like that.'

'Or, if I may remind you, not to bump other men's boats. Steer clear of Stefano's de luxe affair. He'll go up in a cloud of flames if you so much as scratch his paintwork.' Burne grinned disarmingly.

'Perhaps we could take out some kind of insurance in case of accidents,' suggested Felicity.

'I'll attend to that for you,' promised Burne.

He and Trevor went for a trial run in the *Violetta* next day and pronounced the boat a safe buy. Trevor was wildly enthusiastic about the deal.

'He really does know boats inside out,' he told his sister during the evening. 'He gave me lots of instruction about the engine, told me what to do if it suddenly failed, and all that. I suppose he's had boats of one sort or another since he was a kid.'

'Probably,' agreed Felicity. For a moment she had a vision of a youthful Burne Mallory sailing toy yachts on a pond, then later messing about with his first real boat. Perhaps he had been just as impatiently headstrong about boats as Trevor was now.

Burne also now undertook the rest of the deal with Stefano, as well as the necessary insurance. 'I always like to see any documents that Stefano puts his signature to.'

'You mean you don't trust him?' asked Felicity.

'Oh, he's all right—I believe. But perhaps not above a bit of sharp practice now and again. He's clever, though. Always manages to be on the right side of the law.'

'Thank you, Burne,' she said. 'It's very kind of you to take so much trouble.'

Hendrik asked a day or so later if she needed an advance on her salary to pay for the boat. 'I could easily let you have a sum on account.'

'Actually, I could do with a few thousand lire. Trevor needs a few extras, such as clothes and so on, and Burne insists that he buy a lifejacket in case of storms.'

She had no scruples about accepting an advance from Hendrik, but she had been on thorns lest Burne should mention the subject and offer her a loan.

When Hendrik advanced her twenty thousand lire, he added, 'Remember to buy yourself a pretty dress, too. Don't spend it all on your brother.'

Trevor was eager to plan all kinds of trips. 'You must come with me on the first one, Flissie,' he promised. 'That's only fair. We'll go to Isola Rondine.'

'As long as you don't capsize on your maiden voyage,' she agreed, laughing. 'D'you think we should buy a bottle of cheap champagne and bang it on the bows?'

'Silly! That's only for launching. You can't do that afterwards.'

'All right. We'll just drink the cheap champagne. Here's to *Violetta*. I wonder who she was.'

'How d'you mean—who she was?'

'Most boats are named by their first owner and often after the girl of the moment. Perhaps Violetta was one of Stefano's girl-friends.'

Trevor laughed with derision. 'All you know! Violetta is the name of one of Stefano's little daughters.'

'I see. How d'you know?'

'Zia told me. She knows all about Stefano's family.'

Felicity considered that Trevor handled the new boat very well and she received a sense of indirect satisfaction that for so comparatively small an outlay she had been able to give her brother so much pleasure.

By now Trevor had discovered for himself or with Tomaso's aid most of the suitable landing places on Isola Rondine and he tied up at the wooden staging where there was a café close by.

121

'Have you been to the island called Lupa?' Trevor asked, as he and his sister sipped long, iced drinks.

'No.'

Trevor grinned. 'I thought Burne might have taken you. Or perhaps he takes his other girls there, Isobel and Luella and the rest.'

'Perhaps he does. Have you been to Lupa?'

'Not actually landed there. It's rocky and the currents are fast, but I know the right places.'

When they left Isola Rondine Felicity advised Trevor not to try to land at Lupa. 'We could circle round it, I expect. What's there? Any kind of village?'

'Not as far as I know. A few isolated houses, vineyards, olive groves, that sort of thing. No use to tourists.'

But in spite of her suggestion he nosed the boat into a cove between rocky shores, clambered out and tied up to an iron stake driven into the rock.

'Tomaso showed me just the place to land,' he told her. 'I probably wouldn't have found it for myself.'

'So you're still on good terms with Tomaso, in spite of not having bought the boat he offered?'

'Oh, sure. No hard feelings, apparently. He's quite useful and I wouldn't really like to offend him.'

They sat on the sun-baked rocks and from here Isola Rossa was a long green-grey shape floating on the sapphire sea, with a cluster of pink and white buildings by the harbour, surmounted by higher ground covered with what looked like pale rusty foliage. The pomegranate blossom was over and Felicity knew that now every tree was speckled with tiny green fruits that would soon become rosy-orange globes to hang like fairy lights from the boughs.

From this aspect Isola Rondine was a purple smudge with only a barren, rocky shore, and it occurred to Felicity that somewhere along that forbidding coast must be the spot where Burne had taken her that first day and compelled her to climb a ladder to the top.

'It's a good life, isn't it?' murmured Trevor, lying on his back, hands cushioning his head.

122

'You mean this—boat trips and holiday atmosphere?'

'M'm, yes, I suppose so. Suits me fine.'

Felicity laughed. 'It might also suit me fine if I didn't have to work at all and had plenty of money for us both.'

'Why don't you——?' he began, turning towards her. Then he sat up abruptly and hugged his knees.

'Why don't I what?' she asked.

'Oh, nothing. We'd better start back, I think.' He moved quickly to the boat and in a few minutes had cast off, heading towards Isola Rossa. Felicity wondered what he had started to say, but dismissed the notion. No doubt he would like her to get a permanent job in these parts, but that, of course, was out of the question. Once again she fell to conjecturing why Hendrik had apparently sought her in the first place. Was it purely because he was a friend of her English employer, Mr. Firth, and needed a reliable girl for a short time? Had it really been arranged by Mr. Firth in some roundabout manner so that Trevor could be placed in contact with Burne Mallory?

Felicity gave up trying to make sense of the problem. The warm, gentle breeze floated through her hair, the outboard engine puttered quietly, the sea reflected a changing pattern of colour lit by the setting sun, rippling mauves and yellows, emerald and aquamarine. Time enough to worry about other people's motives when she and Trevor had to return to England. If Hendrik needed her for six months, half that time had already sped by. It would be more sensible to enjoy the remainder of the time without delving too deeply into issues that could at least be comfortably shelved.

During the next week or so Felicity was aware that Trevor took Zia out for frequent boat trips, for occasionally he let the girl's name slip out in conversation.

'How did you meet Zia in the first place?' Felicity asked him one evening.

'Through Tomaso,' he replied. After a pause he laughed. 'She's very attractive, but you needn't worry about her, Flissie. I've my wits about me and I shan't do anything stupid.'

She smiled at her brother. 'Of course you won't. You just have to be sure that she hasn't too many other hot-headed Italian boy-friends who might be ready to flash a knife at you.'

Trevor roared with laughter. 'You must have seen some odd films in your time, or perhaps you've read too many thrillers. Zia's all right.'

The summer heat increased day by day until Felicity, who thought she had gradually become acclimatised to the Mediterranean warmth, was glad to accept Hendrik's suggestion and take a siesta in the afternoons, working later in the cool evening to make up the lost time.

'It's not sensible to flog ourselves through the hottest part of the day,' he told her.

'Except that you do,' she pointed out.

'Only if I have urgent jobs to do.'

When Burne asked her one evening if she wanted an evening trip in his boat, she hesitated. 'I really ought to be working. Hendrik insists on our resting in the afternoons.'

'You can always get up at dawn and finish the job,' he suggested. 'Most of us do, but if you want to laze in bed half the day——'

'Half the day!' she echoed indignantly. 'Why, I'm up long before seven.'

'Seven!' he repeated disgustedly. 'The whole town has done half a day's work by then. If you were down there you'd see for yourself.' His eyes held that provocative expression she had come to know so well.

'Maybe one morning I'll get up at five and find out the truth of what you say.'

'Well, that's another day. Are you coming tonight with me or don't you want to?'

'Yes, of course I'll come.' She sensed that a definite refusal would incite him to delve for reasons. Since that night at the opening of the new Casino on the mainland, she had fought down those heady emotions that Burne caused in her when he approached, when he spoke. She had succeeded in dealing with the transaction of Trevor's boat on a business footing, even if a friendly one. She had not met him on any social occasions since then; in fact, his spare time seemed to be taken up with Isobel. Now he was inviting her for an evening trip and she needed all her resolution if she were not to fall into the trap of her own unbidden emotions. It occurred to her now that perhaps Burne had invited other of his friends or members of the staff for a boat trip.

When *La Perla* slid out of the harbour with Burne at the controls, Felicity knew that she had been counting on a kind of rescue operation that would not take place. Burne filled his boat with a large party or he took one special passenger. He did not mix his girls.

Halfway towards Rondine Burne said, 'I have one of those parcels to collect from a man there. Remember that other time when you came with me?'

'Smuggling again?'

'Of course. What d'you think the articles are this time?'

'Oh, I made all my guesses on that previous occasion.'

'When my friend, my accomplice, comes, I'll let you into the secret. After he's gone, naturally.'

Felicity laughed. 'I don't want to be *your* accomplice. You might tell me too much.'

'Exactly. That's why I'm telling you now,' he returned calmly. 'If I cut you in on the deal, you can't give me away. You're an accessory before and after the fact.'

She was silent for a few moments. 'If you really were a smuggler, you'd be very successful, I think.'

'What makes you think I'm not a smuggler?'

'I don't know. Perhaps you're not sinister enough.'

'Oh, that kind went out of fashion years ago. Now one has to be unconcerned, develop a façade of being entirely above-board.' After a few moments he added, 'Or could it be that you believe in my innate goodness? You're certain that I could never stoop to any kind of swindling?'

'Just as though I should answer such loaded questions,' she murmured quietly. 'You're only trying to trap me.'

She was aware of the long sustained glance he gave her

then, but he said nothing further until they were off the island of Rondine. Burne shut off the engine and allowed the boat to drift, although he gave an occasional wary glance at the rocky shore in case he drifted too close.

He had smoked through a long, thin cigar, poured drinks for Felicity and himself, and still the man did not appear.

'He's late tonight,' muttered Burne.

'And you'll have the most awful trouble trying to evade the customs patrol or whatever it is that threatens you!' gibed Felicity. 'A timetable in these things is everything.'

Another half hour went by. Then a boat silently appeared out of the shadowed dusk and a voice called softly, '*Signore!*'

Burne answered immediately and Felicity understood that he was saying how late the man had come. He gave a voluble explanation of his delay and once again a square box changed hands. The Italian moved away swiftly, rowing with one oar in the stern.

'H'm. I'll stow this safely below,' said Burne. 'Then we'll shove off.'

After they were well out of earshot of anyone else, Felicity suggested, 'I can only think that the smuggler brings you boxes of those long, thin cigars you smoke.'

Burne laughed, a deep, throaty chuckle. 'Like to bet on it?'

'All right. But only if you'll tell me what the box really contains.'

'So? You're now quite determined to come in with me in whatever racket I'm on?'

'Maybe. No promises about future cargoes, though.'

'Are you lucky in your gambling?' he asked. 'I like to know the hazards before I risk my money.'

'Oh dear! I'm only betting five hundred lire, unless that stake is too high for you.'

'Any stake might be too high for me where you are concerned.'

What did he mean by that? she wondered. But he had already gone below to the cabin. After a few minutes he reappeared. 'The box is open for your inspection.'

Felicity stepped down the companionway. On the table was the box that the Italian had brought. When Burne lifted out the shavings and wrappings, he showed her a number of little ornaments—brooches made of painted shells, small pottery animals, embossed metal ashtrays.

'Souvenirs of Isola Rondine,' she murmured. 'But why the secrecy?'

'The man who makes them has an exceedingly greedy wife. Whenever he has made a consignment of these little toys and taken them to the mainland to sell, she wants *all* the money. Enrico is willing to give her most, but in the end he gets nothing even for a few smokes or drinks. So I now take over the parcels for him and she doesn't get her claws on all the money, but only part of it.'

'Doesn't she suspect that he makes an extra bit somewhere?'

'Probably, but as long as she can't prove it, Enrico and I are safe. I sell them on his behalf to shops at Monte Rubino and elsewhere, I give Enrico the money when he comes on his fishing business to Isola Rossa. Oh, we work it quite well together, I assure you.'

Felicity laughed. 'You see how well you'd succeed in other forms of skulduggery!'

'You've lost your bet,' he reminded her.

'I hadn't forgotten.' She reached for her handbag, but his hand closed over hers.

'Leave it for now. Pay me later.'

He packed up the trinkets into the box and rejoined her on deck some time afterwards.

He refilled her glass with the light white wine they had been drinking and remained silent for some time. His light-hearted, teasing mood seemed to have vanished now that his rendezvous with the Italian had been made.

'I'm glad you decided to come with me, Felicity,' he said, breaking the long silence.

'It's very pleasant being out here on the water on a cool evening,' she answered politely.

'I've had a bad day,' he continued.

'At the clinic?'

'Yes. One must expect failures sometimes. No one can hope to achieve hundred per cent success, but this particular one is unusually distressing.'

'Tell me about it.' She sensed that he needed a sympathetic ear, someone who could listen in terms of human tragedy and not on the level of professional technicalities.

'She's a young Frenchwoman. She was brought to me a month ago with a temporary blindness caused through a car accident. Usually an operation to cure this kind of blindness is routine. It's not simple, but in most cases it can be done successfully.'

He paused for so long that she assumed that for the moment he had forgotten her presence. 'And this one?' she prompted him after some minutes.

'This one was not successful. There's nothing more than I—or perhaps anyone else—can do. She's married to a prosperous businessman, she has one child—and she's probably going to be blind, totally blind, for the rest of her life.'

'But not through any fault of yours.' She was aware that her voice had sounded a statement and not a question.

'Who can say that?' he demanded harshly. 'Admitted that there was a long delay and she ought to have had my kind of treatment much earlier, how can I be sure that I've done the right thing and not condemned her to darkness?'

'But if you did your best——'

'My best wasn't good enough,' he asserted. 'If I'd left her alone, someone else might not have operated in the same way. Someone else might have saved her sight.'

'You can't blame yourself because one patient has suffered,' she said gently.

'No? Then tell me how you'd feel if that patient were your brother. Wouldn't you blame the surgeon who had operated?'

'I don't know,' she admitted. 'But I know there are some kinds of blindness that can never be cured.'

128

He did not reply.

After a while she reminded him of the innumerable cures he had performed. 'Many people have their sight when all they expected was blindness. That includes Trevor, too.'

Once again he had stopped the engine and the boat was drifting placidly well out of reach of rocky shores.

'I once asked you, Felicity, why you came here, why you were running away, and you told me about this man who let you down. What about him now? Your brother need not be your entire responsibility in future. You're free.'

She was startled by his words, but even more by the fact that she had thought so little about Philip since she had been here in the Adriatic. A few times she had remembered his voice, his face, but now even his features were blurred and indistinct. She had received a letter some weeks ago from a girl who knew Beryl, saying that Philip and Beryl were getting married shortly. The news had made no impression on Felicity, except to wish silently that they would be happy.

Now Burne's words had finally established not only the fact that the old wound had entirely healed but that she was gloriously free. Free to love? But that was madness where Burne was concerned.

'Free,' she murmured. 'Yes, I suppose I am. I've got over all that trouble about Philip. He's going to be married soon.'

'No longer grief-stricken?' Burne queried.

'Not now.'

'I wish I could feel the same about the girl I left behind me.' There was such intense bitterness in his voice that Felicity was reminded of that evening when he had taken her to the little inn on Isola Rossa and they had heard a tune which jangled an anguished memory for him.

Now she could not say, 'Tell me about it,' as she had encouraged him to talk about his professional failure. She could only wait for him to talk or be silent as he chose.

She thought he had chosen silence until, after a long pause, he spoke again. 'She was quite different from you.'

'What was her name?' Felicity asked softly.

'Rosalind. Fair Rosalind, but she wasn't. She was dark-eyed and black-haired, full of vitality. She could dance until dawn, then go out riding in a couple of hours, as fresh as a rose. Then she became engaged to my brother.' He paused again and this time Felicity knew better than to prompt him, for his thoughts had gone away from her.

'Michael and I had rarely quarrelled,' he resumed, 'but although I'd never thought of marrying Rosalind, I felt cheated, as though he'd snatched her from under my nose. Until then I'd not taken any girl particularly seriously. I took them out, squired them to dances and so on, but now Rosalind stirred me as no other girl had ever done. I set out to take her from Michael, God forgive me.'

Again he paused and now his arm was around Felicity's shoulders as though he needed a human contact to help him tell his story.

'At first she laughed and treated me like a future brother-in-law, but gradually I wore her down. I made her see that marrying my brother would be a mistake, but marrying me would be heaven itself. At last, she told me that she would break off her engagement, but I was not to tell Michael until she gave me permission. I had to go to London to the hospital where I was working on eye diseases and I waited for Rosalind's promised telephone call. I got the call, but not from her. From Michael instead. Rosalind had been seriously injured in a car crash.'

'Oh, how terrible for you!' Felicity murmured.

'Well, that's the story. She's a helpless cripple in a wheel-chair—and she married Michael.'

'But they're happy?'

'Oh yes. Very obviously. Of course I wanted to marry Rosalind, however crippled she was, but she pointed out that Michael really loved her—and I'd just wanted her because she was going to marry another man. What I shall never know is whether she was sincere about breaking off with Michael and changed her mind after the accident, or whether she had never had the intention of marrying me.'

'And that's what still hurts you?' she queried.

'It may be only that it still hurts my vanity,' he replied slowly.

'Now that she is married and happy, can't you forget?'

'If I hadn't given Michael a wrecked girl for a wife I might, or if I could lose sight of them both, that might help, but in my own family—now you understand that working with Hendrik is my salvation. I've run away from the past as far as I can get.'

'Thank you for telling me,' whispered Felicity.

He held her away from him and stared down at her face. 'There must be something about you that incites one to confess. I've never told anyone before about Rosalind.'

'You can be sure that I shall respect your confidence,' she assured him.

Suddenly he flung himself away from her. Then he turned and gathered her swiftly in his arms. 'Something in you claims me, Felicity,' he said urgently, his mouth only an inch from her own. 'Why did you have to come here?'

'You know all the reasons why I came,' she answered shakily. There was no opportunity to say more, for his lips were on her mouth, then his cheek against hers and she felt as though she were enveloped by a blissful cloud of nothingness in which only Burne was real.

'I love you, Felicity,' he whispered into her hair. Then she shivered slightly. How many other girls to whom he had said those three words? Heaven was sweet while it lasted, but she knew what she had to do to save herself from the madness of grief.

'I wonder if you do really love me, Burne,' she said quietly.

'Why d'you doubt me?'

'When you kissed me just now, you were really kissing Rosalind. She would always be the ghost between us.'

'Not now. Since I met you, I've felt differently about her. I've seen that she is the past—and she's happy—and I still have my future. That future could be with you, Felicity, if only——'

'You said you loved me, but would you want to marry me?'

'What else?'

Her spirits leapt up joyfully. What else mattered if Burne loved her? She was floating on air again, and when she shyly put her arm round his neck and kissed him, it seemed that all the happiness she had ever longed for was in that moment of his returned kisses.

CHAPTER EIGHT

THE day after that strange and exciting evening with Burne in his boat *La Perla*, he had to leave for a week's medical conference in Rome.

'I'll count the days, my darling, until my return,' he had told her as he left her outside the villa.

'I'll come and see you off,' she promised.

'I'm leaving at dawn,' he teased her. 'You'll still be sleeping.'

'I certainly won't!' she replied indignantly. But although sleep evaded her because she was so happy, she fell at last into a heavy doze and when she awoke the sun was streaming across her balcony.

She threw on a dressing-gown and ran out to the balcony, but she guessed that Burne had already gone. Breathing the cool, morning air, she felt that even the atmosphere had changed. All around her was a wild delight that surged through her veins, made her want to shout that she was happy because Burne loved her. At the same time, perhaps it was an advantage that he should be absent for a few days. She could not live on this giddy pinnacle for ever. While he was away she would have a little time to accustom herself to these changed circumstances, to this new world of rapture.

At the same time she must be careful not to betray this delicious secret to the outside world. She remembered Noel's words that her predecessor, Jill, had 'told everyone that she and Burne were engaged . . .' and how angry Burne had been. Let him take the initiative in that respect when he returned from Rome.

Not even to Trevor would she tell her exciting news, for a careless word might spoil everything. Besides, Trevor had not particularly cared for Philip and had seen him as a menace to his own circumstances. It might be prudent to go slowly with Trevor until the boy had some thoughts about a career, or he would again feel that Felicity was deserting him, even though his sight was so much improved and there was every chance that blindness would be avoided.

Felicity worked so hard at Hendrik's reports and other material that she was able to take more free time in the hot afternoons. Sometimes she bathed at the little cove on the far side of the harbour at Rossa. There were shady spots there near the boulders, a small café and usually only a handful of people dotted about. Trevor joined her occasionally when he could spare time from fiddling with his boat. One afternoon he suggested that they need not return to the villa for dinner. 'Let's have a snack or something down here in the town. I don't want to fag all the way up there only to walk down here again.'

'Going out tonight?' she asked.

'Yes, in the boat.'

'All right,' Felicity agreed. 'Where shall we eat?'

'I know a little *trattoria* in a back street. Quite clean and cheap, too.'

Trevor conducted her through several narrow streets, up a flight of steps and down an alley.

'You're not taking me to Gino's, I hope?' she queried.

'No.'

Eventually Trevor found the little restaurant, so small that it held only three tables, but there was a choice of various *pastas*, as well as fish, and Felicity ordered a light meal.

Halfway through their meal, the door opened and Zia entered, wearing a flame-red dress and a nylon stole shot with gold lurex threads.

Felicity had no doubt that the meeting was prearranged and Trevor had known Zia would come here. She greeted the girl politely, offered an invitation to join them in a meal, but Zia said in Italian that she had already eaten.

She drank the wine that Trevor offered and it was then that Felicity noticed the ornate bangles on Zia's wrists, the earrings with shining stones flashing as the girl moved her head.

'Zia lives near here,' Trevor explained. 'I'll show you her house when we leave.'

When the trio left the restaurant, it was obvious to Felicity that Trevor intended to take Zia out in his boat. She knew that he had already taken the girl on several previous trips, so there was probably no harm in an evening sail.

At the harbour she said, '*Arrivederci*,' to Zia and cautioned Trevor not to be too late home, then left them to return to the clinic where she still had work to do.

How much of Zia's new outfit had Trevor bought? she wondered. She might be doing the girl an injustice. Perhaps Zia had bought all her own finery and trinkets out of money she earned.

Next day Felicity asked casually, 'Trevor, what does Zia do? For a living, I mean?'

'She helps in a shop,' he answered, but the colour intensified in his face.

'Oh? What sort of shop?'

'One of those souvenir and trinket places down by the harbour,' he replied quickly.

'I must go down there some time and buy something from her,' she said smoothly, but left the subject alone.

In August the island was slightly more crowded, for a few Italians came there on holiday, although there was little tourist accommodation apart from one small hotel. Felicity supposed they took rooms in the various restaurants or cafés or else private houses.

Trevor seemed to have plenty of energy and on several occasions he told Felicity that he had taken out passengers in his boat for fishing trips or just around the islands.

'Shouldn't you have a licence of some sort?' she queried, slightly alarmed at the notion. 'It's plying for hire or whatever the authorities call it.'

'Nobody seems to mind here,' he reassured her.

'All right, provided you don't take any risks.'

135

'Stop worrying!' he exclaimed. 'Anyone would think you were fifty-four instead of twenty-four.'

So she tried not to feel apprehensive about this wayward brother until the morning when Isobel said at lunch-time, 'Felicity, I don't want to upset you, but you ought to know that your brother didn't return last night.' Isobel's face was serious and sympathetic.

'Was he out in his boat?' At once all Felicity's alarm rose to the surface.

'Someone could find out if his boat is missing, too. Shall I ask Noel if he'll go?'

'No, I'll go myself,' declared Felicity. 'I ought not to have let this happen. It's that darned boat.'

'Let Noel drive you down to the harbour,' suggested Isobel. 'No need to walk in this heat. If he isn't available I'll drive you myself.'

'Thank you, Isobel. You're very helpful.'

Noel was immediately willing, particularly when it was Isobel who was asking him a favour even if on behalf of someone else.

At the harbour and in the cove there was no sign of *Violetta*, nor of Tomaso, Forto and other acquaintances of Trevor.

'Zia!' exclaimed Felicity. 'Trevor said she worked in one of these shops.'

But there again she drew a blank, for some shops were shut for *siesta* and at the others no one knew of Zia Tonelli.

'But Trevor told me where she lived, if only I can find the house.' She realised that Noel was patiently tramping by her side. 'Look, Noel, don't bother now. Thanks very much for driving me down here. I'll go on looking.'

'I'll ask Mariano on the way back if he knows anything,' Noel promised.

Where was the house? Felicity had only the vaguest notion of the one Trevor had pointed out. She knew it had an outside staircase, but then so did dozens of others in these narrow back streets. Several times she asked passers-by or a woman standing at a doorway where Zia Tonelli

136

lived. At last one man pointed to a house. Felicity thanked him and hurried towards it. To her surprise and, perhaps, relief, Zia herself was idly leaning over the upper balcony of the staircase.

Felicity had to repeat her questions several times, for Zia obtusely failed to understand the other's halting Italian.

At last the girl smiled her comprehension. Trevor had gone fishing last night with other men. That was quite natural, wasn't it? Men fished at night.

A woman's voice from somewhere at the back of the upstairs rooms shrieked out a question. Zia took Felicity's arm and gently urged her towards the stairs. '*Vada! Vada!*' Felicity needed no dictionary to know that she was being hurried away. 'Trevor *bene*,' added Zia as a grain of comfort.

In the street Felicity glanced up and waved. '*Ciao!*' called Zia, and Felicity answered her with a similar '*Ciao!*' that could mean anything.

Fishing, thought Felicity as she retraced her steps, lost herself once or twice, but finally found her way back to the harbour. Then why couldn't Trevor have said so? He had probably been afraid that either Felicity or Burne would prevent him from being out at night. Yet Zia had known.

Felicity returned to the villa where she lived. On the way back she had left a message at Mariano's bar to the effect that if anyone saw Trevor back from fishing, would they please ask him to come up to the clinic immediately?

It was after dinner when Trevor returned and Felicity guessed that he had come back then only because he was hungry and needed a meal.

'It isn't fair to Sofia to give her the trouble of keeping a meal for you or preparing something else when you come in so late,' Felicity reproved him.

'Oh, don't start your scolding tactics,' he begged.

'I wasn't going to.'

'Yes, you were. You want to know why I stayed out all last night.'

'But I know,' she told him. 'You were fishing with

137

Tomaso and the others.'

Trevor's face brightened. 'That's right, I was.'

'Did you have a good catch?'

'Fine.'

'What sort of fish?' she queried, only half believing his tale.

'No idea. Big ones, little ones, all sorts, whatever comes into the net.'

'Oh, I see. You throw out a net.'

'Not exactly. The idea is for several boats to position themselves at the right spot where there's likely to be a shoal. Then Tomaso or someone else gives me one end of the trawl and moves away a short distance, so the net is between us. Then we both move forward and the fish can't help themselves.'

'Then Tomaso and the others land the fish in their boats. What about you? D'you get a share of the proceeds?'

Trevor's face clouded. 'Of course. I've already had a few hundred lire on account, but I've more to come. Tomaso's promised.'

Felicity sighed. She wouldn't exactly trust Tomaso's promises.

'All right. Don't let them make a fortune out of you. Also, if you're going to be out at nights, I think you might tell me. I shan't have to worry about you then.'

'Or go down to Zia's place and ask nosy questions about me,' he flared out.

'She told you, then?'

'Of course. She wasn't too pleased, either. Flissie, don't treat me like a kid all the time. I'm too old to be tied to your apron strings now.'

Felicity smiled. 'As you say, you're old enough now to stand on your own feet.'

Trevor finished his meal and Felicity thanked Sofia again. When the pair were outside the villa, Trevor said suddenly, as though he had been nerving himself for the effort, 'Can you lend me some money, Flissie?'

The word 'Lend' was not meant to be taken seriously

with Trevor, for he had no resources of his own yet. 'How much?' she asked.

'Ten thousand lire would do nicely.'

'But I gave you ten thousand only a week ago. Have you spent it all?'

'I'm afraid so. It doesn't go very far. I can't let the others constantly buy me drinks and so on. Ten thousand anything sounds like a fortune, but it's only a few pounds in sterling.'

Felicity guessed that he was spending money on finery and trinkets for Zia, but at this juncture she would not tax him with it.

'All right, I'll manage it, I expect,' she agreed, 'but, look, Trevor, this is all you get until the beginning of next month, so go carefully.'

His young face lifted hopefully. 'Thanks, love. I won't splash it too much. Besides, soon I shall have more from Tomaso.'

'Don't involve yourself in too many of these night-fishing trips,' advised Felicity. 'You still have to take care and it seems easy enough to get a knock on the head in the dark. Just don't take the wrong risks.'

'No, I promise I won't do anything daft.'

She was glad that next day her brother took the opportunity to have a long sleep and did not leave his room until after lunch.

'How about swimming in the cove?' he suggested when he came to Felicity's balcony where she was stretched out in a cane chair.

'Not so soon after a meal,' she answered, 'but I'd be ready in about half an hour.'

She wondered if Zia was to join them, but if the girl really worked at a shop then ostensibly Zia would not be free to lounge about on sandy beaches in the afternoons.

Trevor's boat was in the harbour and he suggested that he could take Felicity by sea to the cove and tie up there.

'But we could walk across the land in ten minutes,' she objected.

'Ah, but think how cool you'll be in the boat. I can tie up

to the wooden staging and then, if we fancy it, we can go out for a sail after we've swum.'

She let him have his way, for there was little point in arguing. She noticed when he had pulled off his shirt and stood, a slender figure in maroon shorts, how tanned he had become. This long spell in a Mediterranean island should surely set him up in health and provide him with resistance to ailments when he arrived home in London.

After swimming, Felicity bought a packet of chocolate and some biscuits at the nearby café on the beach.

For some time brother and sister lazed in the shade of a large boulder. Trevor munched the biscuits, then stretched himself luxuriously on the sand.

'I could stay here for ever,' he murmured happily.

'We've been over all that before,' Felicity sleepily reminded him.

'No, but seriously, Flissie'—Trevor sat up and a more urgent note came into his voice—'I don't really see why not.'

'Well, you'll have to do something with your life. What d'you think of going in for?'

'I can't see myself sitting in an office nine to five. I wouldn't mind if it were something to do with boats.'

She rolled over towards him. 'Trevor, you'll have to regard boats as a hobby, a pastime. There must be something you wouldn't find too boring.'

He did not answer and she continued, 'Besides, I have to find the money to pay Burne's fees.'

'Didn't Hendrik say you could do that on the instalment plan?'

'He did, but it's still a debt that has to be wiped off, either here or when we're home again.'

She felt a twinge of meanness as she spoke. Her own future was still uncertain and for the time being she had to maintain with Trevor the pretence that eventually she would return to her job in London. Burne's fees were still a debt of honour.

Trevor traced sand patterns with his fingers. 'That's

what I mean. I reckon if you set your mind to it you could easily bowl over Burne. If you were sweet to him, you could twist him round your finger. He'd forget all about his bill then.'

Felicity was momentarily angered, but when she spoke her voice was casual. 'You really think so?'

'Sure. Better still, why don't you marry him? Then we'd all be able to stay here for ever and ever and have the time of our lives.'

'You mean *you*'d have the time of your life! And how d'you propose I should set about entangling Burne so that he'd marry me?'

'Coo!' exclaimed Trevor inelegantly. 'You're not as dumb as that. You managed to hook Philip. I know he got tired of waiting, but that was different. You could use the same tactics on Burne and he'd be a much better catch.'

'I wonder what his reactions would be,' she murmured dreamily. Tomorrow Burne would return from Rome and she might possibly tell him of this conversation.

'You're a fool, Flissie. You're not bad-looking——'

'Thanks a lot.'

'—and it could be that Burne might be ready to settle down with someone not too spectacular. He's that sort of chap. I reckon you've a chance. It would be a splendid thing for both of us.'

Felicity laughed unconcernedly in spite of her mixed feelings of secret happiness and irritation that she could not yet disclose frankly to Trevor what the position was. Yet it occurred to her that until she saw Burne again she could not be certain that she was now his 'only girl'. She could not let her brother know just how much she longed for the 'splendid thing' to come true for all three of them, Burne, Trevor and herself. She took refuge in a flippant response.

'I must see what I can do to ensnare Burne in a web of sweet deception. Be nice to him, you advised. I'll try that, but if it doesn't work——'

'You can save yourself the trouble, can't you?' came an immediately recognised voice behind them.

141

Felicity and Trevor started up as though they had been bitten by crabs. Burne stood leaning on the boulder, his dark golden skin contrasting with his black swimming trunks. At that moment, looking up at him with consternation in her dark blue eyes, Felicity thought he had never seemed so handsome.

'So you were listening!' accused Trevor, turning his embarrassed face away.

Felicity tried to speak. 'I—I—I don't know what you heard, but——'

'I came home a day earlier—for reasons that I believed you might have understood.' His voice was steely and his eyes dark and glittering with cold anger. 'I was told you might be down here on the beach. I'm glad I came after all.'

Felicity struggled to her feet. 'Burne!' she pleaded. 'Why won't you believe the truth? It was a harmless conversation——'

'And it wasn't intended for you,' broke in Trevor.

'I don't need to be told that,' was Burne's jeering answer. 'I'll go now and leave you and your brother to have further conversations about your future plans. But you can rub me out of your diary.'

He stalked away down the beach to the staging and now Felicity saw that Burne's boat *La Perla* was tied up there only a few yards from Trevor's *Violetta*.

For a time Felicity was too frozen to speak. In silence she and Trevor watched Burne step into his boat and move quickly away and out towards the open sea. Not one backward glance had he given to the stricken pair on the beach.

Suddenly Felicity was crying, hiding her face in her arms as she lay on the sand.

'I'm sorry, Flissie,' apologised Trevor in a low, contrite voice. 'I suppose I was talking carelessly, but I'd no idea that he was eavesdropping.'

'You've spoilt everything for me—for all of us,' Felicity said brokenly.

'How? I don't understand. D'you mean that——'

She sat up and brushed aside the tears. 'No, it's not your fault really. It's as much mine. I should have taken you into my confidence, but I didn't. I thought it was a wonderful lark, and now it's shattered in pieces in my hand.'

'So Burne was already getting fond of you? That's what you mean?'

'You could call it that. He said he wanted to marry me. That was before he went to Rome. Now he'll never believe that I wasn't pretending to love him in return. I wish to God I didn't love him!' she finished in a low, anguished tone.

'If only I'd known,' began Trevor humbly.

'If only—life's mistakes inevitably begin like that,' she said sharply. 'If only we'd seen his boat, if only I'd known he was due to return a day earlier, if only we hadn't let our stupid, careless tongues run away with us——'

Trevor put out his hand towards her wrist. 'Don't take it to heart too much, Flissie. Maybe it'll all blow over and he'll be as right as rain in a day or two, treat it all as a joke.'

'Can you see Burne Mallory treating it as a joke?' she demanded. 'Let's go back to the villa. How I'm ever going to face him again I really don't know.'

Trevor scrambled to his feet. 'Well, I do sincerely hope that I haven't spoiled things for you. You deserve a good break with a decent man.' He gathered the towels they had been lying on and shook them free from sand. 'Anyway, perhaps he wasn't the one after all. Who knows? You might meet someone you like much better.'

Felicity forced her stiff facial muscles into the semblance of a smile. Trevor meant well and she had no right to blame him for something he could never have foreseen.

'I'll walk up to the villa,' she decided. 'Then you can bring the boat round to the harbour when you want to. Later, if you wish.'

'I might take Zia out somewhere,' he muttered. Brother and sister needed to be separated from each other for a while and Felicity recognised that Trevor's need for other company was equal to her desire to be alone.

She worked in Hendrik's office for a couple of hours, then went to the villa for dinner, hoping, almost praying, that Isobel would be absent. Fortunately only Luella was there, and since she spoke little English, she and Felicity need exchange only the merest polite remarks. As soon as she could escape, Felicity went to her room. Tonight she needed to be quite alone to mourn the lost chance, the might-have-been. For a short time a door had stood partly open, giving her a glimpse of a shining future, and she had inexcusably, if not deliberately, slammed it shut.

Sleepless, yet weary with self-recrimination, she cursed her own careless tongue even more than Trevor's innocent incitement. Yet might not that same careless tongue eventually rescue her from years of misery? Trevor might be right. Suppose she said 'yes' to Burne and then he was swayed by another pretty face? How could she yield to him, only to be abandoned and deserted when he grew tired of her?

Yet she knew that for all these would-be comforting thoughts, nothing would ever be the same again between her and Burne. The fragile fabric of the dream had been torn to tatters.

She wondered next morning how she could have the strength to meet him without breaking down into an embarrassing scene, but for some days their paths did not cross.

She regretted that she had not discussed Burne's fees for Trevor's operation long before this. Now, more than ever, something had to be done. She could not leave such an important matter in abeyance.

Hendrik had told her that the best way would be for her to transfer money in London, instead of fiddling with foreign currency.

'Burne will name his fee in sterling,' Hendrik assured her. 'Then it will be easy. If you haven't enough in London, your friend Mr. Firth will arrange for a transfer.'

She decided to visit Burne's office in his clinic one morning.

'I will speak to him,' the secretary told her.

In a few moments Burne appeared. 'My fees will be arranged through Hendrik,' he said, so coldly that his words hurt her like a whiplash. 'That was understood at the time, before you came here, Miss Hilton.'

A rush of tears dimmed her eyes and she could only say chokingly, 'Very well. I'll settle with Dr. Johansen. Thank you.'

He had gone back to his own office before she had even finished speaking.

She controlled herself and handed the secretary an envelope. 'Will you give this to Mr. Mallory later, please?'

Inside was a five-hundred-lire note, in payment of the bet she had lost that night on his boat over the 'smuggling'. She had lost a good deal more than the amount of the bet, including her self-respect.

She walked out into the grounds now as though dazed. How could she remain here working for Hendrik and support this ice-cold barrier between her and Burne? Yet she was bound to stay. Trevor still had weekly treatments and checks on his progress. She could not bring herself to desert Hendrik who had been so kind to her. She resolved that she would wear a mask so concealing that not even Burne could see through it.

She had underrated others, though, including Isobel.

'What's happened between you and Burne?' asked Isobel one evening point-blank when the two girls were on Felicity's balcony. Isobel had ostensibly come to borrow some eye-shadow, but Felicity knew that was only an excuse.

'Between me and Burne?' echoed Felicity. 'What could happen?'

'Oh, I thought you were hitting it off very well indeed,' replied Isobel calmly. 'That is—until he went off for that conference in Rome. While he was away you were so

145

absurdly gay that I thought you were relieved to be without him.'

'Was I so gay?' asked Felicity.

'Oh, yes. He spoke about it on the morning he left. I went down to the shore to see him off.'

Felicity's heart skipped a beat. Isobel had gone to see him off at the harbour! What must Burne have thought of her, Felicity, when she had not even troubled to rise early enough even to wave to him from her room balcony?

Isobel was speaking again. 'He said you seemed so different now that your brother's eyesight was improving.'

'Different? In what way, I wonder?' put in Felicity.

'Oh, you laughed more, I think he said. Still, I know only too well how difficult he is. He's the sort that tucks you under his arm, takes you up to a mountain-top, shows you his kingdom—then—wham!—drops you down like a hot potato.'

In spite of herself and the efforts to maintain control, Felicity laughed. 'I don't know where you'd get hot potatoes on top of a mountain.'

'Oh, plenty of places. All over Switzerland, Austria—all the mountain resorts. Don't take me so literally.' Isobel smiled in the most friendly manner, but her next words poured icy water over Felicity's attempt at being casual.

'Thanks, pet, for the eye-shadow. I'll buy some for you next time I go to Monte Rubino. I must fly now. Burne's waiting for me.'

Felicity did not move. She managed to say, 'Good night, Isobel,' in a quiet, croaking voice that she hardly recognised as her own. Then when she judged Isobel to have reached the ground floor, Felicity cautiously peered over the balcony. Isobel was in the driving seat of Burne's car and Burne himself entered as Hendrik walked close by. Burne leaned across and gave Isobel a light kiss, then waved to Hendrik as the car drove off.

How much of that incident was stage management? Felicity wondered. That light greeting kiss—was that for Hendrik's benefit? Perhaps Felicity had been entirely mistaken in imagining that Hendrik loved Isobel. Burne could easily be right in saying that Hendrik was wholly dedicated to his medical work.

Then, too, there was Noel, who not only sensed that even friendliness had vanished between Burne and Felicity, but was openly dismayed that Burne was now once again monopolising Isobel's company.

Noel suggested one evening that Felicity might like to dance at *L'Aragosta*. There was no sense in spending all her free time moping, so she accepted.

'I thought you and Burne were——' Noel began when they were sitting out in the open-air café for a rest between dances.

'Yes? What about Burne and me?' she queried.

'Well, I thought——' He broke off, then continued even more diffidently, 'He seemed to spend quite a bit of time with you. You haven't scorched your wings, have you?'

Felicity managed a light laugh. 'Nothing so damaging. You told me yourself that Burne takes up first one girl, then another, so I mustn't take him too seriously. The answer is that I haven't. A few outings with him don't really count.'

'Sensible girl,' he commented. 'Remember what happened to Jill. Personally, I don't want you to streak off for home before you need go.' He looked moody. 'I wish to heaven that some girl would really count with him, so that he'd leave Isobel alone.'

'Oh, Noel!' she laughed again. 'I thought you were really paying me a compliment in not wanting me to go home, but I was wrong.'

His face lightened. 'Yes, I wasn't very flattering, was I? Sorry, but I'm so tangled up with Isobel that I don't always realise the drift of what I'm saying.'

Felicity remained sympathetically silent. She knew now the truth about the one girl who had really counted with Burne. The girl in England who was still real to him while all the girls he met and danced with and kissed were only shadows.

Sometimes it seemed to her that if one girl were ever

really to take the place of that lost Rosalind, then it would be Isobel. Isobel, with her attractive looks, her charm, her medical training which enabled her to share Burne's professional interests; she was the girl most likely to capture Burne's roving heart, quite possibly because she did not seem to try too hard. When Felicity had been taken out by Burne, Isobel had not displayed any kind of jealousy. If she had felt nettled or irritated, then she had successfully hidden those feelings.

Hendrik, too, evidently had sharper perceptions than Felicity had given him credit for. When she had worked particularly hard during one week, he praised her work ungrudgingly.

'If you would like it, you could have a week's holiday, you and your brother, if he has permission,' he suggested one day. 'You need not spend it here. You could go to the mainland. Monte Rubino has a couple of good hotels, one or two smaller places, and you could explore more of the country from there. You might even take a trip into the Abruzzi mountains.'

'But how will you manage?' she asked. 'Oh, I don't mean I want to sound as though I'm indispensable.'

'Of course not.' His fair face creased into a smile. 'None of us is indispensable, we know. Someone always dings that into us, sooner or later. I thought I might go away for a week or so myself. I've never explored all those islands on the Yugoslav side of the Adriatic. There are so many that one could spend a lifetime pottering in and out and still never know them all.'

'In that case, I'd be glad to go away for a few days,' she said quietly. 'I'll ask if Trevor may come, too.'

Hendrik walked about his office and looked out of the window. His back was towards her when he spoke again. 'This is a very self-contained community here in the clinic and we need to get away from time to time. When we come back the stresses and strains that seemed so enormous to us have shrunk down to their normal size.'

He was telling her in the kindest way that he knew about

148

her hopeless position with Burne. Perhaps he understood her heartache because he, too, had to stand by and watch Burne and Isobel together on the most congenial terms.

'Thank you, Hendrik,' she said in a low voice, not looking at him, for the tears were not far from her eyes. As he passed her chair, he put out a comforting hand on her shoulder and bent to whisper an equally comforting remark in her ear. What he would have said Felicity had no chance of knowing, for at that moment Burne entered the office and stood there, challenging, arrogant, a fierce expression on his dark features. He turned ostentatiously to shut the door and when he turned towards Felicity and Hendrik, he said silkily, 'I'm sorry if I interrupted you, Hendrik.'

He ignored Felicity and she busied herself with the papers on her desk, but rancour almost choked her. How dared Burne put his villainous construction on a purely friendly gesture? His own standards were so low that he used them as a yardstick for other men's motives. She would certainly take that holiday and hope that by the time she returned, Burne would have gone home and that she might never see him again.

CHAPTER NINE

When Felicity suggested to Trevor that they might take a short holiday on the mainland, he seemed less than delighted.

'I'm all right here,' he told her. 'Suits me. Life's one long holiday—while it lasts.'

She laughed a trifle grimly. 'I'm glad you added that last bit—"while it lasts". Sooner or later——'

'Yes, I know, I'll have to look for a job. Still,' he added after a pause, 'you might need a holiday. Why don't you go for a week somewhere?'

'I'm not keen to go alone. I thought you might like to see something more of Italy while you have the chance.'

'True. You fix up something, then.'

'I shan't arrange anything in advance. We'll go to Monte Rubino and then up the coast and inland as well. We can probably stay nights in simple *tavernas* and eat picnic lunches. The whole affair need not cost much.'

Trevor agreed, but a couple of days before the date Felicity had arranged he suggested suddenly that she should accompany him on a trip to Isola Rondine.

'I don't know if I can spare the time,' she demurred at first, but finally gave in, for she had already persuaded her brother to leave his boat in Rossa harbour while they were away on the mainland and today he probably wanted a last trip for the time being in his beloved *Violetta*.

She had not bargained, however, for the arrival of Zia who stepped confidently and obviously by invitation into the boat when Trevor was ready to cast off. Felicity's first impulse was to decline to be the other passenger and step smartly ashore, but second thoughts showed her that Trevor would be so annoyed if she were rude to Zia that he would refuse to co-operate over the holiday. By that time, he had already started the engine and the boat was well away from the harbour wall.

Zia was wearing an obviously new dress of yellow and white patterned cotton, gilded hoops swung from her ears and the soles of her white sandals were almost unscratched.

Had Trevor's money bought these new clothes for the girl? Felicity wondered, but she tried to be as friendly to Zia as she could although she distrusted her very much.

When they landed at Isola Rondine Felicity assured the other two that she did not mind in the least if they wanted to go off on their own. 'I can easily amuse myself down on the shore.'

'Oh no, you must come with us. I've something to show you,' Trevor declared.

Felicity caught a strange quick warning look from Zia and an almost imperceptible shake of the head, but Trevor was insistent and Zia said nothing.

The three walked up the zigzag cliff path in a direction unfamiliar to Felicity. They passed occasional ruined old houses and the road was rough and strewn with boulders and lumps of stone masonry.

'I hope there's something good to show me after this climb,' she said jokingly to Trevor.

'We're here,' he said, stopping outside the ruins of a small stone house. The gaps where windows had been were boarded roughly and several new strips of wood had been used to mend the door.

Zia pushed the door open and invited Felicity to step inside. Coming out of the dazzling sunlight into semi-darkness, Felicity could see little at first, but after a few moments she made out a room with a rough wooden table, a chair or two and a tattered old rug on the stone floor. Nevertheless, the shack was unexpectedly clean; a few wood ashes on the open hearth surprised Felicity, for she had not imagined that at this time of year in so warm a climate anyone would have needed to light even a small fire.

'What is this place?' she asked Trevor.

'It's an old house—or part of it—that once belonged to Zia's grandmother,' he replied. 'No one lives in it now, so Zia has cleaned and smartened it up. A sort of cottage of her own.'

Zia produced a bottle of wine from a box in a corner, glasses from a shelf, and offered drinks to the other pair.

Felicity raised her glass and murmured, *'Grazie.'* Even in the dimness she could see the coquettish glances that the Italian girl slanted to Trevor, and when she had finished her wine she made an excuse to walk outside the ruined old shack. The place had a sinister air, she thought.

She sat down in the shade of a straggly bush to wait for the other two. She could hear Zia laughing, then speaking in rapid Italian to Trevor, who would not understand half of it, but as the two came through the door and Trevor stopped to fasten it, she heard Zia say in Italian that it was a mistake to bring the 'seester'. Trevor understood that and answered in English, 'Don't worry. Felicity's all right.'

Then they saw her as she rose to her feet to join them on the stony, dusty track down the cliff path.

Of course it was a mistake, thought Felicity. Three was no company at all on such an excursion. She was the intruder, although she had no desire to encourage the friendship between her brother and this Italian girl who had such a beautiful face and so sly a manner. A short holiday away from Zia might do Trevor quite a lot of good.

Hendrik accompanied Felicity and Trevor to Monte Rubino by the ferry on the morning of their departure.

'I have to hire a car to go to Vasto to catch a steamer from there to the other side of the Adriatic,' he explained. 'If you fancy staying there for a day or two, I could take you and Trevor,' he offered.

'Thank you, Hendrik. That would fit in very well, for we could then make our way back by easy stages,' Felicity was glad of the chance to save money in fares one way. Also she wanted to get Trevor farther away from the town of Monte Rubino, which was very handy for a quick dash back to Isola Rossa and she knew he hankered all the time to go

152

everywhere by boat.

Hendrik helped to find a clean, comfortable little hotel and pointed out a couple of modest *trattoria* where she and Trevor could eat inexpensively.

Hendrik's steamer left soon after midday and it was early evening before Felicity and Trevor roused themselves to stroll about the town. Originally a Roman town, the centre was a huddle of narrow streets, medieval churches and what looked like a palace. But Felicity was more charmed with the exquisite colouring of the buildings, red tiles capping the rosy brick houses rising in tiers against the blue sky.

A cool breeze invited the whole town, inhabitants and visitors alike, to stroll along the streets and across the piazzas.

At the restaurant Felicity found that fish dishes were the speciality, as they were in Monte Rubino, but here there was a delicious fish stew of shellfish, prawns, squid and many kind of nameless fish.

Three days in Vasto sped by like a dream with mornings on the beach under an umbrella, or spent in exploring the town and climbing to the headlands from which a panorama of a wide sandy bay stretched under one's feet.

The local tourist office suggested a drive into the mountains and Felicity tried to remember every aspect of magnificent scenery to recall when she went back to England.

On the way back to Monte Rubino the tourist office arranged a detour so that she and Trevor could visit the Foresta Umbra, a great expanse of beech and oak at an astonishing height of about three thousand feet. They stayed the night in a small mountain chalet and next day descended through the limestone heights of Rubino down to the town.

It had been an interesting week, thought Felicity, but now they had arrived at Monte Rubino, Trevor chafed to get back to Isola Rossa, so instead of staying a night or two in the town, they took the evening ferry to the island.

Trevor left Felicity at the harbour to attend to his boat. 'I'll come along later,' he promised.

She went across to Mariano's bar to leave the suitcases to be called for later.

'What's the news?' she asked him.

'*Così, così,*' he answered with a shrug. 'Nothing. Only so-so.' He poured her coffee and added cream.

It was strange, she thought, that Mariano had no news. He knew all the island gossip. But at the villa Felicity almost reeled under the impact of one item of news.

Noel met her in the grounds and for once his face was wreathed in smiles as he asked how she had enjoyed her holiday, then promised to fetch her suitcases up later.

'Mallory is going at last,' he told her.

'Going? Where?'

'Back to England. And am I glad to see the back of him?'

A week or so ago Felicity had been eager for Burne to move right out of her life. Now, in spite of all her good resolutions, she could not bear the thought that after a few days she might never seen him again.

'Oh? When is he going?' she managed to ask with some semblance of indifference.

'No date fixed. You know Burne. He likes to make a mystery of everything, as though we'll all be in suspense. When the time comes, I'll make sure we give him a good send-off.'

Perhaps it was only natural that Noel should see Burne's departure as a reason for rejoicing, but she could feel only an agonising longing for Burne's friendship, if nothing more. Then a ray of hope occurred to her. Surely she might find some way of meeting Burne again in England when she, too, had returned.

'Apparently he isn't staying in England,' Noel continued. 'He's thinking of taking up an appointment in Canada.'

Noel's words soon extinguished that tiny gleam of hope.

'Canada?' she echoed flatly. 'Oh yes. Well, it's hardly likely that he'd stay here for ever.'

She escaped from Noel as soon as possible. In her room she relaxed on the bed, but she could not disguise the fact

154

that however far away Burne's profession took him, she would always love him. The thought filled her with humiliation and shame and perhaps some time in the future she would learn to regard Burne as an experience, a memory of wild delight and bitter anguish. Time would undoubtedly cloak both the sweetness and the sharp pangs, and in the meantime she must meet Burne with a mask of indifference.

She did not see Hendrik until the following day when he returned from his trip. They exchanged comments about their respective holidays and Felicity was prepared to put in extra hours, she said, to catch up with the work.

'No need for that,' said Hendrik. 'We shall get through.' He spoke heavily as though he had a problem on his mind. Perhaps it was merely reaction after a holiday, she thought.

Her first meeting with Burne was disastrous. She saw him coming along the private path that led from the grounds towards the harbour. If possible she would have avoided him, but there was no chance of that, for he came towards her with a smile.

'Enjoyed your holiday?' he asked.

'Yes, very much. Every bit of it.'

'Hendrik, too, I hear.' There was an almost menacing glitter in his eyes.

'Yes, I think so. He says he did.' She could not help her words being stilted and unnatural.

Burne shrugged. 'Good for Hendrik. I don't know whether you need the warning or how you'll take it, but don't take Hendrik too seriously.'

'Why should I?'

'No?' His smile was tantalising. 'Others have—and come unstuck. He's not the man for you—but there it is—if you've decided, why should I interfere?'

Hot anger rose within her like a tide and she felt her cheeks flushing furiously. 'Why indeed should you interfere? What business is it of yours? Hendrik at least treats me like a human being. He doesn't come round corners spying on me or——' She broke off, aware that this was probably exactly the scene he wanted. He wanted to humi-

155

liate her, rouse her to raging indignation.

He stood there silently amused, the corners of his mouth curved upwards. Then he said, 'I really believe that sparks shoot out of your eyes when you're angry.'

She ignored that remark and said calmly, 'I hear you're leaving soon for Canada.'

'Oh, you know that, do you? I suppose my departure can't be too soon for you?'

'I didn't say that, but I wish you the best of luck.'

'Thank you,' he answered with exaggerated emphasis. 'I'll remember that.'

She stepped aside and with a hurried ''Bye,' continued her walk along the path to the clinic. She longed to turn her head and see if he were watching her or had gone on his way, but she resisted the temptation. She must learn to be indifferent.

Yet total indifference was stretched to the limit of impossibility when she casually heard that Isobel was soon leaving the clinic and going to Canada.

Canada! That could mean only one thing. Isobel was marrying Burne and travelling with him.

Yet when the two girls met, Felicity thought that Isobel's mood was hardly that of the happy bride-to-be. She seemed taut and anxious.

'Do I congratulate you and give you my best wishes?' Felicity asked rather diffidently, although the words cost her a tremendous effort.

'Oh, this Canada business,' replied Isobel offhandedly. 'Well, I never intended to stay here for ever. I'm not sure just when I shall be leaving.' She walked away hurriedly as though she did not want to discuss the matter, and Felicity had no desire to know too many details. Her imagination could supply enough of those.

In a way perhaps it was fortunate that a new problem cropped up. Trevor followed his sister one day after lunch when she went to her balcony for her usual rest before resuming work. He stretched himself in a long cane chair and said after a while, 'Flissie, I want to talk to you.'

'Yes? What is it?'

He cautiously peered towards the next balcony, then came close to his sister. 'It's about my boat,' he whispered.

'You've damaged it or something?'

'Nothing like that, but when I went down to the harbour this morning my boat had gone.'

'Gone?' she echoed.

'Yes. I asked several people I knew slightly if anyone knew anything or whether she had slipped her moorings. No one had any information. Then I saw Forto bringing it in. I waited for him to land and then I asked him why the devil he'd taken it without my permission.'

'What did he say?' asked Felicity.

'He gave me some yarn about borrowing it for a trip to Rondine and back because his own boat was out of action. I was pretty mad about it and told him not to do it again without my knowledge.'

'Perhaps it was only an isolated incident.'

Trevor frowned. 'No, I don't think it was. In fact, Forto practically let the cat out of the bag. I've strong suspicions that all the time we were away on the mainland Tomaso or some of his pals were using my boat for passenger trips and so on. I wish now that I'd taken *Violetta* with me at least to Monte Rubino and parked her there.'

Felicity was aware that it was she who had dissuaded him from doing just this because she had been afraid that he would return too soon to Isola Rossa.

'There's another thing,' Trevor continued. 'At various times I've brought small parcels over from Rondine or Lupa and delivered them to Mariano's bar to be called for. I'm wondering now what was in the parcels.'

Felicity instantly remembered Burne's mysterious packages.

'D'you think some of your fishermen friends are using you and your boat for illegal business of some kind?'

He grunted. 'I don't know. It's all very well to be obliging, but I don't want to be mixed up in anything shady. I can't be sitting in the *Violetta* night and day. Still,

I'll keep my eyes open. I was intending to go fishing with Tomaso and the others tonight, but I don't think I'll risk it.'

Felicity was gratified by her brother's sensible attitude. At least he recognised danger when he saw it and would not willingly plunge into it for the sake of excitement.

Trevor stayed at the villa for the rest of the day and evening, but next morning he set off for the harbour.

'I'd like to know if someone's been up to any monkey tricks,' he explained to his sister before he went. 'I've thought up a kind of trap to see if anyone else uses *Violetta* when I'm not there. I can soon see if my scheme has been disarranged.'

When he returned in the late afternoon he told Felicity that the boat had apparently not been disturbed.

'I saw Tomaso, though, and I was glad of that. I taxed him about using my boat and he neither admitted nor denied it, but I told him I wanted a share of the money he'd taken. Actually, he owes me some other amounts.'

'And what did he say to that?'

Trevor grinned. 'He said he'd pay me tonight. I'm to meet him at Gino's. Well, that fits in with my plans, for I promised to meet Zia there at about nine.'

'Zia!' exclaimed Felicity. 'Then I'm coming, too. That girl's not to be trusted.'

'Oh, rubbish! Zia's as honest as the day. She wouldn't be mixed up in anything shady.'

'I'm still coming with you,' decided Felicity. 'Tomaso seems rather too hasty to pay you what he owes. I suspect a trap.'

'If you really think it's a trap, then that's all the more reason for your staying away,' argued Trevor. 'Besides, what sort of trap could it be? I can't prove anything unlawful. You're taking it all a bit too melodramatically.'

Felicity, however, insisted on going, although she was dismayed that after dinner Trevor set off without her and she had to catch him up.

'I thought you weren't keen on Gino's place,' he said.

'I'm not. I've been there only once and it looked a rather dubious place.'

'You're wrong there,' he retorted. 'It just happens to be the place where most of the locals go. Nothing wrong with it just because it doesn't set out to attract the tourists.'

She was relieved that she had been able to accompany her brother, for she was not quite sure where Gino's was situated, but Trevor knew the way unerringly.

'Have you been here many times?' she asked him, as they mounted a stair-street with houses darkly forbidding on either side.

'Quite often. It's improved my Italian, if nothing else.'

In the café there was no sign of either Tomaso or Zia and a waiter pointed out an empty table.

'Too early,' Trevor guessed. He ordered some wine and looked about to see if any of his other friends were there.

After about a quarter of an hour, Tomaso came over to the table and asked politely if he might join them.

'*Certamente,*' said Felicity.

He brought with him an almost full bottle of wine and began to refill all their glasses.

'*Alla vostra salute!*' exclaimed Tomaso, raising his glass towards Felicity first, then Trevor.

Felicity acknowledged the toast, but she could see that Trevor was anxious to get down to business. Perhaps, she thought, he had the best of reasons for getting the transaction finished before Zia came in.

'Shall we settle the money, Tomaso?' he asked quietly.

'*Si, si.*' But before complying, he signalled a waiter to bring more wine.

Trevor glanced at his watch. It was nearly half past nine and Zia had not yet appeared.

In a leisurely manner, Tomaso took a scrap of paper from his pocket, wrote a few figures and handed it to Trevor.

'O.K.?' he asked.

Trevor nodded, counted the lire notes that Tomaso handed over and put them away in his pocket.

'*Grazie,* Tomaso.' Trevor seemed pleased by the amount as he raised his glass to the other man.

Felicity was relieved, for she had certainly not wanted her brother to be involved in any kind of scene or commotion.

A few moments later Zia appeared just inside a door close to Trevor's table. She was wearing a striking orange cotton dress, skimpy enough to enhance her full figure.

She gave Trevor a provocative smile, but her expression was sullen when she noticed Felicity.

'You bring the seester, then?' she said to Trevor, in English.

'Well——' began Trevor, as he rose and walked the step or two towards Zia.

'Come with me,' said Zia, beckoning Trevor to follow her out of the door.

Felicity frowned. Then she turned back to Tomaso. 'Where does that door lead to? Another room?'

He nodded. Felicity's uneasiness increased, although she tried to tell herself that there was nothing unusual in a girl wanting to speak privately to a young man.

But the minutes went by and when Trevor did not return, Felicity jumped to her feet with a sense of urgency.

She rushed to the door, half believing that Tomaso might hinder her. She was not in another room but in a dark, evil-smelling passage where she groped her way along until a glimmering light showed a flight of steps with a door at the bottom. When she pushed it open she was out in the open air in a small yard. There was no sound and no sight of Trevor or Zia.

High walls stretched on all sides, but eventually she saw a gleam of light under a door on the far side. At other times she would have been too timid to march boldly into other people's houses, but there was no time now to be diffident. She tried the handle, found the door unlocked and cautiously opened it. She was now in some kind of wine-cellar. Barrels on stands were ranged along one wall and there was a pervading odour of wood and wine.

160

A stout man entered from the opposite direction and exclaimed, *'Che cosa desidera?'* Naturally he would ask what she wanted.

'Scusi, signore. Niente. L'uscita.' She tried to make it clear that all she wanted was the exit.

With a suspicious frown, he pointed to a passage and she fled, almost stumbling up a flight of steps. At last she was in a narrow street, but certainly not the one where Gino's swinging pomegranate lanterns indicated the entrance.

She knew only that this part of the town was higher; therefore she must obviously descend if she wanted to find her way to the harbour and the more familiar neighbourhood.

Ought she to return to Gino's, however, and find if Trevor had returned with or without Zia? She hesitated, but she was not really sure how to find Gino's again.

At the harbour she paused in the shadows, trying to plan what to do next. Mariano might know something, she thought.

He shook his head when she asked if he had heard of any fights or scuffles near by within the last hour.

'Quiet as a churchyard,' he said solemnly.

She leaned across the bar and whispered, 'If you see or hear anything of my brother, could you telephone me at the clinic?'

'He is in trouble?'

'Oh no,' she replied lightly. 'It's only that I missed him at the place where we were to meet,' she added.

Leaving Mariano's, she went down to the harbour wall. Now it occurred to her that perhaps she was taking all these little events far too seriously. Fight or scuffles? Why would anyone pick quarrels with Trevor—unless it were over Zia, perhaps? On the other hand, it could be that all Zia wanted was an evening trip with Trevor in his boat.

Unfortunately Felicity had no idea exactly where Trevor's boat might be tied up and it was difficult to recognise or see the name of a particular boat moored to the wall. She walked back round the harbour wall to the cove where there was a wooden staging. She picked her steps down towards the shore, but there was enough reflected light from the town to show her that no boat was moored to the staging.

It had not occurred to her to be frightened of prowling around lonely beaches in the dark, but when she saw a man's shadowy figure move towards her she scrambled quickly to a more illumined part of the tiny promenade that was no more than an extension of the harbour wall. She went into the garden café of *L'Aragosta* and quickly out again, hoping to throw off any pursuer, then hurried up to the villa as fast as she could go.

She was panting breathlessly by the time she reached the clinic grounds. All her hopes were centred on finding Trevor safely there. Instead, Burne was sitting in the porch.

'Have you seen Trevor?' she asked.

'No. Should I have?'

'I must find out if he's in his room.' Without waiting to give an explanation she rushed up the stairs, but she had really known in her heart that Trevor would not be in the villa, either in his own room or in hers.

She stood for a few moments on the balcony of her room. What on earth could she do next?

Burne called to her, 'What's the matter? Come down and tell me.'

She realised that she was silhouetted against the light behind her and she went back into her room and closed the windows. She felt numb with fear. She ought to be doing something positive to find Trevor, but what? In her mind she retraced the events from the moment when Trevor had gone out of the café with Zia. She had made a mistake there. She should have had no scruples about butting in on her brother and the girl.

With some reluctance she went downstairs and out of the villa. Burne was still waiting at the spot from which he could see her room.

She told him now of Trevor's suspicions about his boat

162

being used, his meeting with Zia and the fact that Tomaso had paid him some money.

'Much money?' queried Burne.

'I'm not sure. Whatever the sum was Trevor seemed very satisfied.'

'Well, what makes you think that something has happened to him? He's probably only gone off to a quiet spot with this girl Zia.'

'I've just a feeling that this appointment with Zia was planned, a kind of trap, and she knew Trevor would have that money on him.'

'And you think he might have been attacked. Then we must try to find him. I don't want even an accidental blow to upset all the work I've done.'

In her present distraught mood Felicity's anger flamed.

'Is that all you can think of?' she demanded hotly. 'He's just a case to you, an interesting case, and you hope nothing will happen to destroy your work.'

'Don't you also share that hope?' he asked quietly.

'D'you need to ask? It's as much your fault as anyone's that Trevor has possibly been landed in trouble. You encouraged him to get a boat——'

'I certainly did not encourage him too much,' Burne snapped. 'In his madcap craving for a boat, I chose what I thought was the least of all the evils. Otherwise, he'd have been out in anybody's boat, getting himself mixed up in God knows what scrapes.'

'Well, I can see quite plainly now that all that business about Stefano letting him have a boat was all a put-up job. Trevor was offered one particular boat by Tomaso, and at the very moment he almost offers to buy it Stefano comes along at exactly the right time, according to plan, no doubt.'

'A put-up job it may have been, but not by me,' declared Burne. 'When I heard that Stefano was involved I did my best to inspect the boat and see that Trevor had at least a sound craft that wouldn't sink when he was out in the open sea.'

'I still wonder if you're not involved with some sort of racket yourself.' She threw the words at him. 'All that pantomime about collecting parcels of souvenirs from the man on Isola Rondine, tales about his greedy wife. That might have been a very innocent plant! Maybe under those brooches and ashtrays were more important goods.'

'Such as?' he enquired, dangerously grim.

'Oh, I don't know! Whatever the local people find profitable.'

Imperceptibly he had drawn her into the shadow of the clump of cypress trees under which was a stone bench. He forced her to sit down, then sat beside her, still holding her shoulders in an iron grip.

'If you believe that I'm involved in some illegal game, then your best plan is to go straight to the police.'

Her anger was spent and she could make no reply.

'If I say that what you need now is a night's sleep, will you snap my head off?' His voice was gentle and warm and it proved her undoing, for she suddenly and ashamedly broke into a flood of tears.

'That's better,' he consoled her, offering her his handkerchief. 'You don't let yourself cry often enough.'

Her head was on his shoulder and his arms had closed around her, and for a few sweet moments she longed to stay that way, but she forced herself to recover some of her self-control.

Burne and Isobel were soon going to Canada—together. They had evidently made up their minds and Felicity must remember that Burne's caresses, even in an emergency, were not really meant for her. She pulled away from him.

'Don't worry too much about Trevor,' Burne advised her. 'By the morning you may find he's come home after all and no damage done.'

'You make it all sound very simple.'

'Then ask yourself what more can you do until tomorrow morning.'

She sighed as she rose from the bench and walked towards the villa entrance. 'I'd better go in,' she said flatly. 'Anyway, if I'm out here with you at this time of night Isobel won't like it at all,' she reminded him.

'Isobel?'

'Yes. You're—sort of engaged to her, aren't you?'

In the dimness she could not see his face. 'Good night, Felicity,' he said abruptly, and walked quickly out into the grounds.

As she wearily climbed the stairs to her room her tired mind could only assume that Burne wanted to keep his engagement secret for the time being.

CHAPTER TEN

FELICITY sat on her bed for a long time before undressing. She tried to comfort herself with the thought that Trevor had merely changed his mind and gone out fishing with the other men.

She lay in bed at last, but sleep was far away and towards dawn she decided to go down to the harbour again. She took the precaution first of looking into Trevor's room, but there were no signs that he had returned. She left the villa as inconspicuously as possible and fortunately she met no one in the grounds, although usually even at this early hour many of the staff were about.

At Mariano's she stopped for a cup of coffee.

'You are early here, *signorina*,' he remarked.

'Yes, I have a lot to do today,' she answered. She did not know how far she could trust Mariano, although she had always found him helpful and honest.

'You have seen your brother?' he asked quietly.

'No,' she answered casually. 'But most likely he went out fishing last night with the other men. He'll return later.' After a few moments, she said, 'Mariano, do many people have parcels left here for them?'

'*Si, si.* Many people on Rondine or Lupa or Monte Rubino.'

'Why?'

Mariano shrugged and spread his hands. 'Cheaper that way. If people send on the ferry-boat, they must pay, so everyone helps with the parcels in their boats.'

The explanation sounded plausible enough, and as though to confirm Mariano's words, three men entered the café and set down a small sack and two boxes. Then they demanded coffee and breakfasts and Mariano hurried away to serve them.

166

On her way out of the café Felicity read the addresses on the packages. One was for Mariano himself, the other two bore addresses of other parts of the Island.

She hoped for Trevor's sake that the parcels he had brought across were equally innocent-looking.

She had already planned to call at Zia's house. If it were true that the girl worked at a shop, she would leave fairly early. Felicity doubted, however, whether Zia worked anywhere at all. That was only a tale that Trevor had told to cover up for the Italian girl and make it sound plausible that she bought her own clothes and trinkets.

Once again Felicity had difficulty in finding Zia's house among the maze of back streets and when she arrived she was accosted by an older woman, whom she took to be Zia's mother.

'Zia Tonelli,' Felicity said, making it clear in her halting Italian that she wanted to see Zia at once.

The woman showed her along a narrow passage, up some creaking stairs and into a small bedroom.

Only a hump of bedclothes betrayed the occupant of a small black iron bedstead.

'Zia!' called Felicity, and the hump stirred.

Felicity called again more imperatively and the girl rolled over and thrust out a tousled head.

Zia blinked her eyes and yawned. 'Oh, the seester!' she muttered, and rolled over with her back to Felicity, who refused to be defeated so easily. She shook Zia's shoulder with some vigour.

'Listen, Zia. You asked Trevor to meet you at Gino's. Why?'

Zia turned over and began to giggle. 'You speak bad Italian,' she said in her own language.

'Very likely,' admitted Felicity, 'but you know the truth. You asked Trevor to meet you. What happened after you went out of the café with him?'

Zia sat up and shrugged her beautiful shoulders. 'You want to know? Your brother is not here—now.' She added that last word with sly insolence.

167

'Then was he here last night?'

Zia's mouth widened into a grin. 'That is something I do not answer.'

'Well, never mind last night. Where is he now?'

'How should I know?'

'If you don't tell me where he went,' Felicity persisted, 'I shall go to the police.'

Zia flung back her head and laughed with high amusement. 'The police! One is my brother!'

Felicity was nonplussed for the moment. Zia might not be speaking the truth about her brother, but that could be determined later.

'Even if he is your brother, it is his duty to try to find missing persons.'

'What is a missing person? Maybe Trevor went out in his boat somewhere and he has not returned.'

There was nothing more to be gained from Zia, and Felicity was glad to get out of the house and into the fresh air. The girl's bedroom had been filled with an offensive stuffiness, a blend of cooking smells and cheap scent. As she hastened down the narrow streets, under the arches and down innumerable steps, Felicity realised that Mariano had been right in not encouraging Zia to frequent his café. She did not for one moment believe that Trevor had spent part of last night or any night with Zia. That was only another sign of Zia's vain bravado.

At the harbour Felicity inspected every boat moored there. In daylight she could see the names clearly, but there was no trace of the *Violetta*. The quayside was now piled high with boxes of pomegranates, the first early crop of the season, waiting to be shipped to the mainland. The rosy orange fruits, tough-skinned and shiny as an apple, would be a lifelong memory of these past few months on Isola Rossa.

A woman at a nearby stall held several pomegranates in her hand, inviting Felicity to buy. '*Melagrane?*' she offered.

'*Grazie,*' murmured Felicity as she took three and paid

for them.

She wondered now what next she could do in her search for Trevor. She could not comb the entire island, still less the other islands. It seemed that no one could help her unless she called in the police. She asked herself why she was so reluctant to approach the police and realised that she was still not sure whether Trevor might somehow be implicated in some unlawful activity, even though he was undoubtedly innocent. Yet she must do something.

From Mariano's café she telephoned Isobel and asked if Trevor had returned to the villa.

'No. Has he been away?'

Felicity gave the briefest explanations and Isobel promised to keep a look-out in case she heard or saw anything of the boy.

From her view through Mariano's window Felicity now noticed that Burne's motor-cruiser *La Perla* was not in its usual place, although sometimes he tied up at the cove past the harbour. Had he already joined in the search or was he off on some pleasure trip of his own?

She ordered more coffee and buttered rolls and as Mariano set down the cups and plates at her table she heard him give a sharp exclamation.

'What is it?' she queried. She stood up and gazed through the window across to the quay.

'The *guardia* is talking to Forto.' Mariano shook his head sorrowfully. 'Fortunato is his name, but he is not lucky, that one.'

The two men seemed to be talking on amiable terms.

'Did Forto come ashore from a boat?' Felicity asked Mariano.

'*Si, si.*'

'Does Forto often have trouble with the police?'

Mariano shrugged. 'He is always doing things the *polizia* could catch him for.'

Then Forto and the policeman smiled at each other and parted.

In a sudden flash Felicity dashed out of Mariano's and

169

across the road. If Forto had landed from his boat, then he had either come from one of the other islands or the open sea. He might know something about Trevor. At least he would know whether the boy went fishing last night.

But Forto had disappeared by the time Felicity reached the quayside. Had he seen her coming and vanished before she could question him?

She looked about for the *guardia* to whom Forto had been talking, but he, too, was nowhere in sight.

It occurred to Felicity that a visit to Isola Rondine might do no harm. It was just possible that Trevor might have gone to Zia's ruined old house on the island. Inactivity was leading nowhere and in the meantime Trevor might be in the utmost danger.

As she had to wait for the midday ferry that linked the three islands and the mainland she now returned to Mariano's to eat the rolls she had ordered. Mariano brought her a hot cup of coffee and enquired sympathetically, 'You see Forto? Was anything wrong?'

She shook her head. 'No. I lost sight of him.'

When she arrived at Isola Rondine she searched every foot of the beach and peered inside the café before starting up the zigzag path that led to the ruin, but somewhere she must have missed the way, for the path climbed even more steeply and became more overgrown than she remembered. She pushed through some bushes and found herself near the peak of the island crowned by the ruins of an old fortress.

Exhausted by the heat, she sat down to rest for a while before descending the path. The afternoon had become sultry and it seemed from the hazy appearance of the sea that thunder might be approaching. She was thirsty and remembered the pomegranates she had bought, but when she cut one open it was barely ripe, for evidently the fruit was picked early enough to allow for delay in transport. Still, the sharpness of the pippy flesh made her throat less dry.

She scrambled down the way she had come and tried again to find the right track. She approached the old shack which she thought was the one and walked cautiously

170

around the outside. There was no sound from inside. The door was shut and she tried to peer through a crack in the boarded window openings, but she could see nothing but intense darkness. She called softly, 'Trevor!' but there was no answer.

Screwing up her courage, she boldly opened the door and peered into the gloomy interior. There was no sign of anyone. She returned down the dusty path, avoiding the limestone boulders, and went to the beach café to think out what next to do. She felt angry with herself. She had come here on a wild-goose chase when all the time Trevor might be safely at the clinic or in the utmost danger elsewhere.

She would have to wait for the evening ferry to return to Isola Rossa and all she could do now was to keep a look-out for any boat she recognised.

The sea was still and mistily grey, the sky an oppressive blanket with the sun scarcely visible. Since she had been at Rossa, there had been practically no rain at all, but she had been told that once the autumn storms started, the downpours were startling and drenching.

After a snack at the café she went to a corner of the crescent-shaped beach where she could sit in the shade of a pine tree. The spot disturbed her, for it was here that she and Burne had sat, so long ago it seemed, when he had taunted her with running away from her problems in England.

She refused to think of Burne, but reflected that had she waited this morning he might have been able to help her. At least he had his boat available. But after those angry accusations, of which she was now thoroughly ashamed, she could scarcely expect his help. Besides, he had his own work and responsibilities at the clinic.

Her eyes closed, partly with the sultry heat, but probably more because of fatigue and strain of the past twenty or so hours. She woke with a jerk, remembering that she must not miss the ferry. She realised she was shivering. Wide awake now, she saw that the beach was entirely deserted, the umbrellas taken in; not a single boat bobbed at the side

171

of the wooden staging. The ferry! Her watch indicated half past six and the ferry had gone long ago.

She scrambled to her feet, collected her belongings and hurried towards the café. To her astonishment it was closed. Yet when she had been here late in the evening in Burne's boat, the café had surely been open. Perhaps it was shut now so that it could open later.

She gazed wildly around, but there was no one in sight, no one to ask if there might be another boat or one that could take her back to Isola Rossa. She was completely marooned.

Now with the approaching storm the daylight was fading fast and a few large drops of rain splashed down. She must take shelter before the worst of the storm started, but suddenly sheets of rain poured down, the heavy drops bouncing in the sand and throwing up little fountains of dust. She ran towards a small wooden building that sold ice cream and managed to crouch down on the lee side. In the distance she could hear thunder and once she saw jagged forks of lightning on the horizon.

In spite of the meagre protection afforded by the hut, her clothes were already soaked and she realised she must find some better shelter. She was annoyed that she could not remember in which direction was the house of Signora Lombardo, where Burne had taken her on that first trip to Rondine, but it was a waste of time wandering all over the island looking for it. Zia's ruined shack was nearer and she might even take shelter in one of the other old ruins near by.

The path was slippery although the rain had partially stopped and Felicity was determined this time that she would not take the wrong track. When another violent shower came she stood under a group of trees for a short time. The rain dinned and hissed angrily and then as suddenly subsided. By now the evening was prematurely dark and she approached what she thought was the right ruin.

The door was swinging open in the wind, although she was certain she had pushed it shut when she left. She sidled along the wall, and fear of the unknown nearly compelled her to bolt down the path, but she forced herself to remember that she had come in search of Trevor and it was her own fault that she had been caught in the heavy storm.

She stepped inside the open doorway and held her breath. No rough hand grabbed her or hit her on the head, so she took courage, but in the pitch darkness she stumbled over a wooden case.

There was still silence. '*Chi è?*' she called softly, then again in English, 'Who's there?' Only then she caught the sound of a muffled sigh. For a moment she closed her eyes in terror. Someone was waiting to receive her, someone was hiding in the darkness waiting ... She stumbled again, this time over something soft, a sack or a bundle of rags. She knelt down, then recoiled with a half-stifled scream. She had touched a human hand. Oh, if only she had a torch, a box of matches, anything to give light in this pit of darkness!

She nerved herself to explore timidly this inert body on the floor. Obviously a man; his clothes were damp, so he must have been out in the storm. She shook his arm, felt his face, then called, 'Trevor! Trevor!' trying to convince herself that she had found her brother and not some unknown man.

To her relief, the head moved a little under her touch and the man groaned. Felicity lifted him to a sitting position and supported him by her knee.

'Trevor! Can you hear me? It's Felicity!'

'M'm,' he grunted. Then in a tired voice he repeated, 'F'lic'ty.'

She nearly collapsed with the overwhelming relief of finding her brother, but the next moment she was alarmed again. She did not know if he were injured.

'Are you hurt?' she asked.

'My ankle!' he groaned. 'I fell.'

'Have you any matches?' she asked. 'We need some light.' She hunted through his trouser pockets. 'Where's your jacket?'

'I don't know. Perhaps I dropped it outside.'

Then she remembered that inside her handbag was a small folder of book matches, but they were damp when she tried to strike them until she tried a match on the rough surface of the walls.

She found a stump of candle and stuck it on top of a wooden case.

'What happened? Where have you been all day?' she asked. 'I came up here earlier and there was no one here then.'

'It's a long story,' he mumbled. 'My throat—parched.'

'Plenty of water outside, but I'll see if I can find anything here.' With the aid of the candle she searched around and found half a bottle of wine left over from some previous meeting here.

'Drink this,' she coaxed her brother. 'It might put some warmth into you.'

She also found some dirty sacks which provided rough covering for him.

'How badly have you hurt yourself?' she asked.

'I think it's only a sprain, but it's damned painful,' he muttered.

'How did it happen?'

'It's all mixed up,' he complained.

'Tell me about it from the time you met Zia in Gino's.'

'Oh yes. As soon as we were outside the café and in some street, a couple of chaps came up and told me to leave Zia alone. One of them said she was his girl and he'd knife me if I didn't clear off. At least, that's what I understood. Zia clung a bit to me for protection, but the two men grabbed her and ran off. I started chasing them, but I soon had to give up. They soon disappeared, along with Zia.'

'Yes? What then?' Felicity prompted gently.

'I went down to the harbour. Then I thought I ought to go back to Gino's if you were still there and bring you home, but I met Forto. I asked him if he'd seen anything of Zia and two men. He said he had and she'd gone to Rondine with them. So—oh, I reckon it was a fool thing to do,

174

but I went down to my boat and set off for Rondine. I suppose I had some Galahad ideas about rescuing her from a couple of toughs.'

'But she wasn't here,' Felicity stated.

'No. How did you know that?'

'Because I saw Zia this morning in her own house in bed.'

Trevor sighed. 'What a fool I was!' After a few moments he resumed. 'I slept here a few hours, then when it was daylight I started off down to the shore. I suppose I hurried too fast because I was so mad about everything. When I picked up my jacket I found that every lira had been taken. All that money that Tomaso gave me—my own—everything.'

'Zia probably knew that you'd just received the money from Tomaso,' commented Felicity.

'Of course she knew. I thought Tomaso was being rather generous. Now I know why. I expect Zia gives half of it back to him.' Trevor's tone was full of disgust.

'What happened when you left this place? How did you hurt your ankle?'

'Just went headlong over a boulder. When I got up I could hardly walk, so I lay down in the most comfortable place I could find and must have gone to sleep.'

'How long were you out in the open?' she asked.

'Most of the day, I suppose.'

'That's how I missed you. I was here about four o'clock and the place was empty. Couldn't you have tried to get help?'

'I did. I tried to get towards the shore. I was hungry by then, but I fell twice and bruised my shoulder, I think. Then it started to rain and I knew I had to get back to this place. I suppose I'd passed out by the time you came. What made you come here?'

Felicity explained her hunch about Zia's shack. 'I missed the return ferry and the storm came on, so I thought of this place as a likely shelter.'

'Glad you did, Flissie.' He squeezed her wrist. 'But what

175

now? What shall we do stuck here?'

'As soon as it's daylight I'll go down to find help somewhere and get you to the shore. Where's your boat? I didn't see it at the landing stage.'

'No, it's beached at that little cove on this side. There's a path that comes up the opposite way from the one you took.'

The candle guttered and died and Felicity sat on the floor as close as possible to Trevor, who had fallen into a doze.

It seemed an eternity to daylight, but at last a few faint chinks of light filtered through the cracks in the boards.

'I'm going now,' she told Trevor. 'I must find help.'

He muttered a sleepy reply and she set off yet again down the now familiar path, picking her steps carefully in case she, too, slipped and fell.

When she reached the beach café there were no signs of life, but she met an early fisherman and asked the way to the village. At the first house she came to she asked if there was a doctor on Isola Rondine. The woman shook her head and Felicity explained about her brother's plight. After a consultation with several neighbours, one young man offered to help her.

'*Grazie*,' she thanked him, and led the way to the ruin.

The door was open, but there was no sign of Trevor. She searched outside. The boy could surely not have walked away by himself. Then someone must have taken him. Her fears now struck their greatest intensity. Tomaso or Zia's friends had been here and spirited Trevor away in her absence.

In confusion she thanked the young man who had accompanied her, making an excuse that another friend had helped her brother in the meantime. She found a couple of hundred lire in her handbag and pushed the notes into his hand.

After the man had gone she did her best to tidy her appearance. Her dress, once pale lime-green, was mud-stained and bedraggled, her shoes were quite ruined, but when she looked at her face in her mirror, she was appalled. No wonder the villagers had stared aghast at her, no doubt believing her to be one of the island's legendary apparitions.

In the daylight from the open door she cleaned her face and combed her hair, fighting down the new suspicions that some further harm had come to Trevor. She must get away from this place at once and go down to the beach.

As she took a last look around the shack, she accidentally pushed over an empty case. Bending down to right it, she became aware that someone had entered through the open door. She crouched in the shadows behind another case. Then she felt herself bodily lifted by a pair of strong arms and she yelled with fright. Her assailant turned her to face him. 'Burne!' she exclaimed.

'Who else?'

'Trevor! Where is he?'

'Safe. I took him to a friend's house. Why didn't you stay here, too?'

'I had to get help for Trevor,' she mumbled. Then because she was exhausted with the night's turmoil and lack of sleep and now Burne had appeared to take her to safety, the tension snapped and she burst into floods of tears.

'Cry your eyes out,' he suggested. 'You won't look any worse than before. My darling, you're a sight!'

She mustered a weak smile and lifted her face. Holding her tightly in his arms, he bent to kiss her lips and her tear-stained cheeks.

'Isobel,' she murmured faintly when she could speak. 'You must remember——'

'Damn Isobel!' he said roughly. 'She and I have had a hard time trying to get what we wanted. Come along. You need some dry clothes and I'm taking you to Signora Lombardo. Remember where we had lunch one time?'

Remember? She would never forget each separate and individual outing she had taken with Burne. Those incidents would be strung together like a necklace of of memories.

177

He supported her with his arm down a different path to Signora Lombardo's house. 'If only you'd known the way, you could have sheltered here for the night in comfort,' he said.

In daylight she realised that the distance was very short and she could have gone there for help. Signora Lombardo and two young girls fussed about Felicity, wrapping her in blankets, giving her facilities for washing herself, then supplying her with a new set of clothes.

Trevor was lying on a couch in another room and he, too, looked cleaner and tidier in a borrowed shirt.

Signora Lombardo brought steaming coffee and rolls with butter and luscious jam and Felicity thought a breakfast had never tasted so good.

Two men helped Trevor down to the shore where Burne's boat was moored. The sun shone brilliantly as though the storm had never taken place and, but for the fact that she was wearing borrowed clothes, Felicity almost believed that none of last night's adventures had really taken place.

Trevor remarked, 'To think that this is the first trip I've ever taken in your boat, Burne—and if I hadn't cracked my ankle, I don't believe you'd take me now. Have you seen anything of my boat?'

Burne was casting off the mooring rope and *La Perla* slid away from Isola Rondine heading for Rossa.

'Yes, you beached her very badly and during the storm she drifted away. Luckily, I met someone who'd seen the *Violetta* and taken her in tow. She's over at Rossa now.'

'Thank heavens for that!' muttered Trevor.

At the clinic Trevor was immediately handed over to one of the doctors. 'A simple sprain and a few bruises,' was the verdict. 'A few days' rest and you should be all right.'

Burne disappeared before Felicity could even thank him properly for coming to her rescue, but there were also other matters to be attended to.

In Hendrik's office she apologised for her absence the day before. 'I knew you'd understand how anxious I was about

178

Trevor,' she told him.

'Of course, my dear Felicity. We were all anxious, too.' Hendrik was all smiles and in the gayest of moods. 'Let's skip some of the work today, if we can. You need a rest.'

Could any employer ever be so considerate? she wondered.

She returned to Trevor's room to keep him company for a while.

'Where's Burne?' he asked.

'I don't know. I expect he has a great deal of work to catch up.'

'I wonder why he came over to Rondine,' mused Trevor. 'Was he looking for me or for you?'

'I haven't had time to ask him that yet,' she replied.

'He tore a strip off me for spraining my ankle and letting you go for help. As though I could help doing myself an injury or stopping you from tearing off when you chose.' Trevor grinned. 'I think he's still a bit smitten with you.'

'What nonsense! He has quite different ideas,' she retorted sharply.

Burne came into the room almost immediately and she wondered if he had heard those last two remarks, but if so, he showed no sign.

'How's the ankle?' he asked Trevor.

'Not too bad.'

'Then you don't need Felicity to sit here holding your hand.'

'Why? D'you want her to hold yours instead?' Trevor asked cheekily.

Burne glanced down at the boy. 'There are times when you could mind your own business. This is one of them.'

He almost dragged Felicity out of the room and down the stairs. 'I want to talk to you,' he said, so sternly that she fluttered with apprehension.

'I want to thank you, Burne, for all you did for Trevor and——' she began, trying to put in her spoke first.

'A fine dance you led me!' He grabbed her elbow and hurried her along, out of the villa and into a secluded corner of the garden where the stone bench was almost hidden by a cypress hedge.

'How did you know where to look?' she asked timidly.

'Look!' he echoed. 'I literally had to hunt you down. You dashed off at dawn, leaving no message.'

'I was worried about Trevor,' she defended herself.

'Not half as worried as I was about you,' he scolded her.

She began to feel a rising tide of joy, something that made her breathing difficult, yet in spite of the fact that he had called her 'My darling' when they were in the shack and kissed her so tenderly, she dared not let herself believe that Burne's angry manner meant anything more than a wasted day.

'I scoured the town,' he continued. 'Every café, every place I could think of. Mariano said you'd been in and he thought you might have gone to Rondine, but he didn't know if you had returned. Four times I went to the police and they knew nothing whatever about the "mad English brother and sister." By now it was the middle of the night and I had to cope with a hell of a storm.'

'Oh, Burne! I'm sorry I gave you so much trouble,' she said contritely.

'So you ought to be sorry!' he grumbled. 'Even then when I arrived on Rondine I didn't know if I'd find you or only Trevor. First I went to Signora Lombardo and she had seen nothing of either of you. I searched every one of those damn ruins, including the old fort, until I found your brother. Then *you* were missing. He said you'd gone down to the village for help. I nearly went crazy, wondering if you'd slip somewhere and do something more drastic than spraining your ankle.'

She raised her glance towards him. 'Would you have minded very much?'

For answer he took her roughly by the shoulders. 'You know darn well that I would. Have I been wasting all this time trying to tell you how much I mind? How much I care?'

'But—Isobel—you said——'

'What about Isobel?'

'I thought you were both going to Canada—together,' she whispered.

'I *shall* go to Canada if you won't marry me,' he threatened.

'That's the last thing I want you to do.'

'What? Marry you?'

'No. Go to Canada, unless I come with you.'

He held her in his arms tenderly and kissed the tip of her nose. He laid his not very well-shaven cheek against hers and her arms stole round his neck.

'Poor Isobel,' she murmured sympathetically. 'She said once that I was not your type of girl.'

'She was right. You're not! I've always avoided redheads like the plague. Blondes and brunettes and even the mousy ones I can manage, but you—when you looked at me with those accusing blue eyes of yours—if I'd had any sense I'd have turned and run.'

'Because you hoped I'd run after you?' she mocked.

'Perhaps.'

'I was tempted to sometimes, but I was so determined that I wasn't going to be just another of a long string of girls.'

'You gave me the brush-off very efficiently,' he admitted. 'But tell me now—which end of the string of girls d'you want to be?'

'The one where the knot is at the bottom.'

His laughter rang out in the quiet garden.

'I'm still rather concerned about Isobel,' she said.

'You needn't be. She's getting what she wanted—Hendrik.'

'Hendrik!' she echoed. 'But she said——'

'Oh, Isobel and I had to play a pretty deep game,' he explained. 'Hendrik appeared to be in love with her, yet he could never bring himself to the point. At first, Isobel was only amused, but gradually she came to see that he was the man she wanted. Then he seemed to be married only to the

181

clinic and back he went into his shell. Perhaps that's his Scandinavian heredity. So Isobel and I did our utmost to make him jealous—and you, incidentally——'

'Me?'

'Well, you were really the least important part of our plan,' he jeered, then laughed at her indignation. 'But at least pay me the compliment of pretending you were jealous.'

'All right, I won't pretend. I was *madly* jealous.'

'In the end we both had to pretend that we had been offered posts in Canada. In my case it was true—still is— but we hoped that Hendrik would wake up at last.'

'And has he?'

'To Isobel's delight and my relief, he has.'

For a few moments she remained silent. 'Funny thing,' she said then, 'whenever you go away from a place, even for a day, something always happens. Things are different when you come back.'

'True. I'd rather have today than yesterday. Come on, we'll tell Hendrik and Isobel our ill-kept secret. Neither will be surprised.'

Burne took her to Hendrik's private villa, which Felicity had visited on only rare occasions, for when he was off duty Hendrik liked his solitude.

Isobel was there, wearing a ravishing coral silk dress, and Felicity was glad she had put on a white lace outfit she had bought on the mainland.

'Well, Hendrik, you can pour the champagne now,' commanded Burne. All four drank toasts to each other individually and in pairs.

'Lucky you had me at hand to give you a shove,' growled Burne, giving Hendrik an affectionate push.

'Lucky you had me, too, to create a little opposition,' cut in Isobel, with a mischievous glance at Felicity.

The private lunch party for the four of them was a wild success, although Felicity could not remember what she ate.

'I hope we're all off duty this afternoon,' she said with

mock severity, as Burne refilled her wine-glass.

'We're all going out in Burne's boat,' Isobel told her.

'Are we?' Burne looked comically indignant. 'Who invited you—or Hendrik?'

'We did,' was Isobel's calm reply. Felicity noticed how serene was Isobel's manner. She had lost that tense air, that edginess which sometimes made her appear discontented.

Towards evening the two girls prepared a meal in the galley of *La Perla*.

'I haven't yet thanked you for all you did for me,' began Felicity, but Isobel interrupted with, 'Let's say we gave each other mutual support.'

'You'll stay here with Hendrik, of course, on the island?'

Isobel smiled happily. 'As long as Hendrik finds his work here. If he wants to go elsewhere after a few years, then we'll go together—unless he wants to live in the Arctic Circle. After this Mediterranean warmth I've become soft.'

Felicity laughed. 'You? Soft? Never! You're firm and un-dithery. I'm the one that's soft.'

'You weren't very soft in tearing over to Rondine to look for your brother and venturing into some old ruin, were you?'

'Only because Trevor was involved.'

'Has Burne spoken to you about his own future?' queried Isobel as she set out plates on a tray.

'Not yet. We haven't had a moment to sort things out. Everything's happened in such a rush.'

The moment came later during the evening when Isobel and Hendrik were in the galley cosily engaged in the task of washing-up. The boat drifted lazily in the twilight and Burne sat with Felicity in the bow.

'Will you object to living in England again?' he asked.

'I'll live where you live—just as Isobel and Hendrik will stay together here.'

'It's been a wonderful experience to work here in this isolation and be one of Hendrik's team, but I feel that I ought to be involved again in the rush and pressure of my kind of work. In England I'll take the cases that need

183

whatever skill I have. Here on Rossa only the wealthy can come to me, except for the occasional selected case sent by a group of sympathisers. What do you say, Felicity?'

'I want your work always to be as satisfying as you can make it.'

'We need not live in the heart of London all the time. I have a rather dilapidated cottage in Berkshire where we could spend week-ends or a few extra days in the summer. You can amuse yourself with designing interior decorating for it. There's a garden, if you fancy you have green fingers.'

'It sounds both exciting and peaceful at the same time. I haven't told Trevor our news——'

'I doubt if he wants it spelt out in words of one syllable. He's not that dumb.'

'Then if he's already guessed, that's all right. I think he wouldn't mind if he could get some sort of job in boat-building. Southampton or somewhere like that. Then in his spare time he could sail or just mess about with boats.'

Burne's eyes twinkled. 'I can't say that he's been one of my most docile patients, but between us, we'll manage to turn him into an honest citizen yet.'

Felicity grasped Burne's hand. 'Until now I've never been able to thank you enough for all you've done for Trevor and his future. You must know how very grateful I am for rescuing him from a lifetime of helplessness.'

His hand closed over hers. 'You must never pity the blind or believe they are helpless. Some hidden strength always seems to come to them, so that they overcome their handicap. Still, I'm glad to have saved Trevor's sight—or at least, barring mishaps, I think I have. Give me your gratitude, Felicity, by all means, but gratitude is not what brings warmth to a man's heart.'

'What does?' she asked softly, knowing the answer.

'To hear you say "I love you, Burne".'

It was no hardship to say the words and mean them. The rest of the evening in the starlit darkness seemed like a dream to Felicity. From another boat came the throbbing

184

music of a guitar and then a man's voice singing a full-throated air that echoed over the water. It was a night of magical fantasy that she would never forget. She leaned against Burne's shoulder in utter contentment.

At the end of September Isola Rossa staged a Feast of the Pomegranates, the *Festa delle Melagrane*.

'You must stay for this,' Isobel had suggested. 'It's like the wine festivals they have in Rhine towns.'

Hendrik had also declared that he could not part with Felicity until that time. 'After September I shall not need to tease Isobel by importing another English secretary,' he said with a provocative glance at Isobel.

She laughed. 'Really, Hendrik, I thought you were keen to provide me with an English companion.'

Felicity joined in their laughter. 'Now I know what was going on. I often wondered why you didn't get a competent girl from Rome.'

The arrangement of staying until the beginning of October suited Burne, for he had a number of cases to attend to. 'I can't cancel them just because I've taken up with a red-haired piece,' he told Felicity, ruffling her newly set hair.

Noel Bennett, however, decided to return to England as soon as Hendrik would release him. He gave Felicity his best wishes, though even those were slightly tinged with doubt.

'I hope you'll be happy with Burne,' he said, 'but don't ever let him fool you.'

'I'm sorry about Isobel,' she said gently.

'It's bad luck, of course, but I'd sooner lose her to Hendrik than to—all right, I won't say Burne, seeing that you're determined to marry him. He's not really a bad choice. I suppose I've never been able to see straight because I was crazy about Isobel.'

Felicity saw him off on the morning of his departure and hoped that somewhere in the future he would find the right girl.

For some days before the Festa the streets began to be

prepared with coloured lights, decorative streamers, flowers in window-boxes. Stalls and booths were erected, each owner vying with his competitors for the most attractive design.

In the shops were displays of pomegranates set among clothes or toys or cosmetics or whatever the shop usually sold. In sheds and backyards man-size effigies were being prepared all in pomegranates, often painted in colours to represent fifteenth-century costume.

For two days there were processions and ceremonies, jugs of pomegranate juice freely offered for tasting, dancing at night in the streets, until eventually the whole atmosphere was pervaded with the heady smell of the *melagrana*.

Felicity had watched or taken part in most of the events, usually with Burne except when he was on duty at the clinic. By the evening of the second day she was practically exhausted with enjoyment.

'I haven't the stamina,' she complained. 'I'm not cut out for these hectic revels.'

She and Burne were sitting in their favourite corner of the open-air café *L'Aragosta*. Throngs of merrymakers roamed the streets, laughing, singing, dancing.

'Remember that this is practically the last opportunity of the year when the people here have money to spend,' Burne told her. 'After the pomegranate harvest, they have to rely through the winter on fishing, the occasional tourist—not many of those—and picking up whatever living they can make on the mainland. Stefano pays off his people now and takes them on again in the early spring. He keeps only the smallest possible skeleton staff for maintenance.'

'The islands should encourage more tourists to come here in the winter,' Felicity suggested. 'The climate is ideal.'

'The government is trying to, but Rossa needs hotels, and they cost money. Not that I want to see the usual matchbox skyscraper here. That would spoil the charm of the islands.'

She was silent for some time and some of the noise from the streets had subsided when Burne leaned across the table towards her. 'I had a letter today from my brother,' he said

186

slowly, almost painfully.

'Not bad news?' she queried.

'No. On the contrary, really good news. My sister-in-law, Rosalind, has had two more operations and at last she's able to walk. Not very easily yet, but there's hope that eventually she'll be normal. The doctors say she may even dance, if she's patient and willing to go slowly at first.'

'Oh, Burne, that *is* good news!' The bitter burden he had borne for so long seemed to lift from her own shoulders.

'She added a postscript—here, read it for yourself.'

He thrust the sheet towards her and by the light of the swaying coloured lanterns, she read the few words. 'You were not at fault in the first place. Now you know that you need never blame yourself in the future. Bring Felicity to see us as soon as you can. Love, Rosalind.'

There were tears in Felicity's eyes as she handed him back the note.

'Perhaps your name meant something to me when we first met,' Burne whispered. 'Anyone named "Felicity" ought to bring happiness, but I wasn't sure if I deserved it.'

'But now you know,' she said warmly.

'I may still not deserve it, but I'm darned if I'm going to let the chance sail past me.'

The tide of revellers had receded and Felicity and Burne were the only customers left in the garden café.

'I suppose I shall have to write to my former employer, Mr. Firth, and tell him I shan't be going back,' she said.

'He'll learn to survive without you,' replied Burne unfeelingly. 'But I have to thank Hendrik for getting you here. He's a pal of your previous boss, isn't he?'

'Yes, he is.'

'Then we'll have a final drink to Hendrik. The man who brought you to the island.'

'To Hendrik—and the Isle of Pomegranates.' They raised their glasses and clinked them.

Then they left the café, to the relief of the tired waiter,

and strolled along the harbour wall. An almost full moon slanted a shimmering path across the dark sea, a light or two gleamed on the dim shape of Isola Rondine. Somewhere from the back of the town the music of guitars and mandolins was borne faintly on the breeze and Burne and Felicity, hands clasped, walked in a small enchanted world of their own.

Have You Missed Any of These
Best Selling

HARLEQUIN ROMANCES?

Here are other
HARLEQUIN ROMANCES
you will enjoy